# Maigret and the Millionaires

# Maigret and the

*Translated from the French by Jean Stewart*

# Millionaires

## Georges Simenon

A Helen and Kurt Wolff Book
A Harvest/HBJ Book
HARCOURT BRACE JOVANOVICH, PUBLISHERS
San Diego    New York    London

Requests for permission to make copies
of any part of the work should be mailed to: Permissions,
Harcourt Brace Jovanovich, Publishers, 8th Floor,
Orlando, Florida 32887.

Library of Congress Cataloging in Publication Data
Simenon, Georges, 1903–1989
Maigret and the millionaires.
"A Helen and Kurt Wolff book."
Translation of Maigret voyage.
I. Title.
PZ3.S5892Maegs     [PQ2637.I53]     843′.9′12     74–7009
ISBN 0-15-155143-X
ISBN 0-15-655150-0 (pbk.)

Printed in the United States of America
First Harvest/HBJ edition 1986
B C D E F G H I J

# Maigret and the Millionaires

*What
was happening
at the Hotel George V
while the rain was falling over Paris,
Maigret was asleep,
and various other people
were doing their best to sleep also*

"The most frustrating cases are those that seem so run-of-the-mill that at first you don't think they're important. It's like those illnesses that sneak up on you, beginning with vague discomfort. When you finally take them seriously, it's often too late."

Maigret had once said this to Inspector Janvier one evening when they were returning together to the Quai des Orfèvres over the Pont-Neuf.

But on this particular night Maigret made no comment on the events taking place, because he was sound asleep beside Madame Maigret in their apartment on Boulevard Richard-Lenoir.

If he had expected any trouble, it would not have been from the Hotel George V, a place more often mentioned in the social columns of the press than among the sensational news items, but rather from the daughter of a minister, a girl he'd called in to warn her to stop indulging in certain eccentricities. Although he had adopted a fatherly tone, she had taken his reproof badly. It's true that she had just been celebrating her eighteenth birthday.

1

"You're just a petty bureaucrat—I'll have you fired."

At three o'clock in the morning a fine drizzle was falling, barely visible, yet just enough to make the street surfaces glisten and the lights glitter as though seen through tears.

At half past three, on the third floor of the George V, a bell rang in the room where a chambermaid and a valet were dozing. They both opened their eyes. The man was the first to notice that it was the yellow light that had just flashed on. "It's for Jules," he said.

That meant a call for the room waiter, who went to take a bottle of Danish lager to one of the guests.

The two servants dozed off again in their chairs. There was a longish pause, then the bell rang again, just as Jules, who was over sixty and had always done night duty, came back with his empty tray.

"All right, all right!" he grumbled between his teeth.

He made his way leisurely to suite 332, where a light shone above the door; he knocked, waited for a moment, and then, hearing nothing, opened the door gently. There was nobody in the darkened sitting room. A little light came from the bedroom, where a faint continuous moaning, like a child's or an animal's, could be heard.

The little Countess was stretched out on her bed, her eyes half-closed, her lips parted, both hands clasped over her heart.

"Who's that?" she moaned.

"The waiter, *Madame la Comtesse*."

They knew one another well.

"I'm dying, Jules. I don't want to. Call the doctor quickly. Isn't there one in the hotel?"

2

"Not at this time of night, *Madame la Comtesse*, but I'll get in touch with the nurse. . . ."

A little over an hour before, he had brought up to that very suite a bottle of champagne, a bottle of whisky, some soda water, and a bucket of ice. The bottles and glasses were still in the sitting room, except for one champagne glass that had been overturned on the bedside table.

"Hello! Get me the nurse at once. . . ."

Mademoiselle Rosay, the operator on duty, showed no surprise, but inserted one plug, then another, into one of the many holes in the switchboard. Jules heard a distant ringing sound, then a sleepy voice.

"Hello! . . . Nurse speaking . . ."

"Will you come down immediately to number 332?"

"I'm dying, Jules. . . ."

"You'll see, you won't die, *Madame la Comtesse* . . ."

He did not know what to do while he was waiting. He went to turn on the lights in the sitting room, noticed that the champagne bottle was empty, while the whisky bottle was still three quarters full.

The Countess Paverini went on moaning, with her hands clenched over her breast.

"Jules . . ."

"Yes, *Madame la Comtesse*?"

"What if they come too late . . ."

"Mademoiselle Genévrier is coming down right away. . . ."

"If they do come too late anyhow, tell them that I've taken poison, but that I don't want to die. . . ."

The nurse, gray-haired, gray-faced, her body still redolent of sleep under her white smock, came into the suite after tapping gently at the door for appearance's sake. She had a

3

bottle of something brownish in one hand, and her pockets were bulging with boxes of medicine.

"She says she took poison. . . ."

Mademoiselle Genévrier took a quick look around, saw the wastepaper basket, extracted from it a pharmaceutical container, and read the label.

"Ask the operator to call Dr. Frère. It's urgent. . . ."

It seemed as though now that there was somebody to look after her the Countess had surrendered to her fate, for she no longer attempted to speak and her moans became weaker.

"Hello! Please call Dr. Frère immediately. . . . No, no, not for me! . . . It's the nurse who's asking. . . ."

These things happen so often in luxury hotels and in certain districts of Paris that at the police first-aid posts, when they get a call from the Sixteenth Arrondissement, for instance, somebody almost always asks: "Downs?"

"Get me some hot water."

"Boiled?"

"It doesn't matter, just so it's hot."

Mademoiselle Genévrier had felt the Countess's pulse and lifted her upper eyelids.

"How many pills did you take?"

A girlish voice replied, "I don't know. . . . I can't remember. . . . Don't let me die. . . ."

"Of course not, dear. Drink this, anyhow. . . ."

She had her arm around the patient's shoulders and was holding a glass to her lips.

"Is it horrible?"

"You drink it up. . . ."

Near by, in his apartment on Avenue Marceau, Dr. Frère

4

dressed hurriedly, grabbed his bag, and presently, leaving the silent building, got into his car, which was parked parallel to the sidewalk.

The marble entrance hall of the Hotel George V was deserted, except for the night receptionist, who was reading a newspaper behind his mahogany desk on one side, and the bell captain, who was doing nothing at all on the other.

"Number 332," announced the doctor as he went by.

"I know . . ."

The switchboard operator had given them the word.

"Should I call an ambulance?"

"I'm going up to see. . . ."

Dr. Frère was familiar with most of the suites in the hotel. Like the nurse, he gave a token knock on the door, then went in, took off his hat, and moved swiftly to the bedroom.

Jules, after bringing a pitcher of hot water, had withdrawn into a corner.

"Poison, doctor . . . I've given her . . ."

They exchanged a few words, like a kind of shorthand or conversation in code, while the Countess, still propped up on the nurse's arm, was retching violently and beginning to vomit.

"Jules!"

"Yes, doctor . . ."

"Get them to call the American Hospital at Neuilly to send an ambulance . . ."

There was nothing unusual about all this. The operator, her headphones over her ears, spoke to another night operator at Neuilly.

"I don't exactly know, dear. . . . It's Countess Paverini, and the doctor's up there with her. . . ."

The phone rang in number 332. Jules answered, and reported, "The ambulance will be here in ten minutes."

The doctor put away the hypodermic he had just used for an injection.

"Shall I get her dressed?"

"Just wrap her in a blanket. If you can see a suitcase anywhere, pack a few things. You know better than I do what she'll need. . . ."

A quarter of an hour later, two attendants carried the little Countess downstairs and lifted her into the ambulance, while Dr. Frère got into his own car.

"I'll be there by the time you are. . . ."

The doctor and the ambulance attendants were old acquaintances. He also knew the hospital receptionist, to whom he said a few words, and the young doctor on duty. These people spoke little, and always as though in code, because they were accustomed to working together.

"Room 41 is free. . . ."

"How many pills?"

"She doesn't remember. The bottle was found empty."

"Did she vomit?"

The doctor knew this nurse as well as the one at the George V. While she organized things, he lighted a cigarette at last.

Stomach pump. Pulse-taking. Another injection.

"Just let her sleep now. Take her pulse every half hour."

"Yes, doctor."

He went down in an elevator exactly like the one in the hotel and gave some instructions to the receptionist, who jotted them down.

"Have you notified the police?"

"Not yet . . ."

He glanced at the black-and-white clock. Half past four.

"Get me the police station on Rue de Berry."

There, bicycles were standing in front of the door, under the lamp. Inside, two young constables were playing cards and a sergeant was brewing himself some coffee over an alcohol lamp.

"Yes . . . Rue de Berry Police Station . . . Doctor what? . . . Frère? . . . Like *brother*? . . . okay . . . I'm listening. . . . Just a minute . . ."

The sergeant grabbed a pencil and jotted on a scrap of paper the information given to him.

"Yes . . . yes . . . I'll tell them you're going to send in your report. . . . Is she dead? . . ."

He hung up and said to the other two, who were watching him, "Barbiturates . . . George V . . ."

For him this just meant extra work. He lifted the receiver again with a sigh.

"Headquarters? . . . Rue de Berry Station here . . . It's me, Marchal. . . . How are things on your end? . . . It's quiet here. . . . The fight? No, we didn't keep them at the station. . . . One of the thugs knows a lot of people, you know? . . . I had to call the superintendent, who told me to let them go. . . ."

There had been a fight in a night club on Rue de Ponthieu.

"Well, I've got something else. . . . An O.D. . . . Will you take the report? . . . A countess . . . yes, a countess . . . Real or phony, I don't know. . . . Paverini . . . *p* as in Peter, *a* as in apple, *v* as in Victor, *e* as in . . . Paverini, yes . . . Hotel George V . . . suite 332 . . . Dr. Frère, like your brother . . .

7

American Hospital at Neuilly . . . Yes, she talked. . . . She wanted to die, then she stopped wanting to. . . . The same old story."

At half past five Detective Inspector Justin, of the Eighth Arrondissement, questioned the night concierge of the George V, wrote a few words in his notebook, talked to Jules, the waiter, and finally made his way to the hospital at Neuilly, where he learned that the Countess was asleep and that her life was not in danger.

At eight o'clock that morning it was still drizzling, but the sky was lighter, and Lucas, who had a slight cold, sat down in his office on Quai des Orfèvres, where the previous night's reports awaited him.

He was thus informed, in a few official phrases, about the fight on Rue de Ponthieu, the arrest of ten or twelve prostitutes, some cases of drunkenness, a knifing on Rue de Flandre, and a few other incidents, none of which were out of the ordinary.

Six lines told him, moreover, of the attempted suicide of the Countess Paverini, *née* La Serte.

Maigret showed up at nine o'clock, still a little worried about the minister's daughter.

"Has the chief asked to see me?"

"Not yet."

"Anything important in the reports?"

Lucas hesitated for a second, decided that, all things considered, an attempted suicide, even at the George V, was not an important matter and answered, "Nothing . . ."

He had no idea he was making a serious mistake that was going to complicate Maigret's life and the crime squad's entire file.

When a bell rang in the hall, the superintendent, carrying a few files, left his office and went with the other departmental heads to a meeting in the police director's room. They discussed outstanding business that concerned the various superintendents, but Maigret said nothing about Countess Paverini because he knew nothing about her.

By ten o'clock he was back at his desk and, his pipe between his lips, was beginning his report on a case of robbery with assault that had occurred three days earlier; an Alpine beret that had been dropped at the scene of the crime would, he hoped, enable him to trace and arrest the criminals very shortly.

At about the same time, in the Hotel Scribe on the Grands Boulevards, a certain John Arnold, who was breakfasting in pajamas and dressing gown, picked up his telephone receiver.

"Hello, mademoiselle . . . Will you get Colonel Ward at the Hotel George V?"

"Right away, Mr. Arnold."

For Arnold was an old habitué of the Hotel Scribe; he lived there almost all year round.

The switchboard operators at the two hotels, the Scribe and the George V, knew one another without having met, as operators do.

"Hello, dear, will you put me through to Colonel Ward?"

"For Arnold?"

The two men habitually phoned one another several times a day, and the ten A.M. call was traditional.

"He hasn't called for his breakfast yet. . . . Shall I call him anyway?"

"Wait a minute. . . . I'll find out. . . ."

The plug shifted from one hole to another.

"Mr. Arnold . . . the Colonel hasn't rung for his breakfast yet. . . . Shall I ask them to wake him up?"

"Has he left no message?"

"I haven't been told of any. . . ."

"It's ten o'clock, isn't it?"

"Ten after ten. . . ."

"Call him again. . . ."

The switchboard got busy once more.

"Call him, dear. . . . Never mind if he grumbles. . . ."

There was silence on the line. The operator at the Scribe had time to put through three other calls, including one to Amsterdam.

"Hello there, dear, have you forgotten my Colonel?"

"I keep ringing him. He doesn't answer."

A few minutes later there was another call from the Scribe to the George V.

"Listen, dear. I've told my caller that the Colonel doesn't answer. He says that's impossible, that the Colonel is expecting a call from him at ten o'clock, that it's very important. . . ."

"I'll try ringing him once more. . . ."

Then, after a vain attempt: "Wait a sec. I'll ask the concierge if he went out."

A pause.

"No. His key's not on the board. What shall I do?"

In his room, meanwhile, Mr. John Arnold was losing patience.

"Well, mademoiselle, have you forgotten my call?"

"No, Mr. Arnold. The Colonel doesn't answer. The

concierge hasn't seen him leave and his key isn't on the board. . . ."

"Get them to send somebody to knock on his door."

The messenger this time was not Jules, but an Italian named Gino, who was on duty on the third floor, where Colonel Ward's suite was five doors away from Countess Paverini's.

Gino called back to tell the concierge: "There's no answer and the door's locked."

The concierge turned to his assistant. "You go and see. . . ."

The assistant, in his turn, rang, knocked, and said softly, "Colonel Ward . . ."

Then he took a master key from his pocket and managed to open the door.

Inside, the shutters were closed and a lighted lamp stood on one of the living-room tables. The light was on in the bedroom too, with the bed turned down for the night and the pajamas laid out.

"Colonel Ward . . ."

Some dark clothes lay on a chair, some socks on the floor, and a pair of shoes, one of them sole upward.

"Colonel Ward! . . ."

The bathroom door was shut. The concierge's assistant knocked first, then pushed open the door. He simply uttered a brief oath.

He thought of telephoning from the bedroom, but felt so reluctant to remain there that he hurried out of the suite, closing the door behind him, and without waiting for the elevator ran down the stairs.

Three or four guests had gathered around the concierge, who was consulting a transatlantic-airways timetable. The assistant whispered in his boss's ear.

"He's dead. . . ."

"One moment . . ."

Then the concierge, realizing the meaning of the words he had just heard: "What's that you said?"

"Dead . . . In his bath . . ."

The concierge spoke to his visitors in English, asking them to be patient for a moment. He crossed the hall and leaned over the reception desk.

"Is Monsieur Gilles in his office?"

On receiving an affirmative nod, he went to knock at a door in the left-hand corner of the lobby.

"Excuse me, Monsieur Gilles . . . I've just sent René up to the Colonel's. . . . It seems he's dead, in his bath."

Monsieur Gilles wore striped trousers and a black jacket. He turned to his secretary.

"Call Dr. Frère immediately. He must be on his rounds. Make sure they get hold of him. . . ."

Monsieur Gilles knew certain things of which the police were still ignorant. So did the concierge, Monsieur Albert.

"What d'you think about it, Albert?"

"The same as you do, I suppose."

"You've heard about the Countess?"

A nod was enough.

"I'm going up there."

But since he felt disinclined to go alone, he took with him one of the sleek-haired, tail-coated young reception clerks. As he went past the porter, who had gone back to his post, he told him:

"Get in touch with the nurse. . . . Send her down to number 347 at once."

The hall was not empty, as it had been during the night. The three Americans were still arguing as to which plane they should take. A newly arrived couple were filling in forms at the reception desk. The florist was at her stall, so was the woman who sold newspapers, next to the theater-ticket agency. Several people were sitting waiting in armchairs, including the head saleswoman of a leading couturier with a carton full of dresses.

Upstairs, on the threshold of the bathroom in suite 347, the manager didn't dare to take a second look at the obese corpse of the Colonel, lying in the tub in an odd position with the head under water and only the paunch protruding.

"Call the . . ."

He broke off on hearing the telephone ringing in the next room, and hurried to answer it.

"Monsieur Gilles?"

It was the operator's voice.

"I was able to contact Dr. Frère at one of his patients' on Rue François Ier. He'll be here in a few moments."

The young reception clerk was asking: "Whom shall I call?"

The police, obviously. In the case of an accident like this it was unavoidable. Monsieur Gilles knew the local superintendent, but the two men didn't get along. Moreover, the local police sometimes behaved with a lack of tact that could be embarrassing for a hotel like the George V.

"Call the Department of Criminal Investigation."

"Who shall I ask for?"

"The director."

They had occasionally been fellow guests at dinners, which, although they had only exchanged a few words, would serve as an introduction.

"Hello! . . . Is that the director of the Department of Criminal Investigation? Excuse me for bothering you, Monsieur Benoit. . . . This is Gilles, manager of the Hotel George V. . . . Something has just happened. . . . I mean I have just discovered . . ."

He was at a loss how to put it.

"Unfortunately a very important person is concerned, a world celebrity. . . . Colonel Ward . . . Yes, David Ward . . . A member of my staff has just found him dead in his bath. . . . No, I don't know anything more. . . . I thought it best to call you right away. . . . I'm expecting the doctor at any moment. . . . I need not ask you . . ."

To be discreet, of course. He had no desire to see the hotel invaded by journalists and photographers.

"No . . . No, of course . . . I promise you nothing shall be touched. . . . I'll stay at the scene myself. . . . Here is Dr. Frère. . . . Would you like to speak to him?"

The doctor, who was still in complete ignorance, picked up the receiver that was offered him.

"Dr. Frère speaking . . . Hello! . . . Yes, I've just arrived, I was at a patient's. . . . What did you say? . . . No, I can't say he was one of my patients, but I do know him. . . . I once treated him for a mild case of the flu. . . . What? . . . On the contrary, very healthy, in spite of the life he leads . . . used to lead, rather. . . . Excuse me, I haven't seen the body yet. . . . Of course . . . I understand. . . . Soon, then, *Monsieur le Directeur* . . . Do you want to speak to him again? . . . You don't? . . ."

14

He hung up, then asked, "Where is he?"

"In the tub."

"The head of the Department of Criminal Investigation says he's sending somebody over and nothing is to be touched in the meantime."

Monsieur Gilles spoke to the young reception clerk:

"You can go down again. Keep a look out for whoever comes from the police and see that they're sent up quietly. . . . No gossip about this in the hall, please . . . Is that clear?"

"Yes, sir."

A bell rang in Maigret's office.

"Will you come in here a minute?"

It was the third time the superintendent had been disturbed since beginning his report on the robbery with assault. He relighted his pipe, which had gone out, crossed the hall, and knocked on the chief's door.

"Come in, Maigret. Sit down."

A little sunshine was now mingling with the rain and gleaming on the brass inkstand on the chief's desk.

"Do you know Colonel Ward?"

"I've read his name in the papers. He's the man with three or four wives, isn't he?"

"He was just found dead  n his bathtub at the George V."

Maigret remained unmoved, his mind still on the hold-up.

"I think you should get down there in person. The doctor who's more or less attached to the hotel just told me the Colonel was perfectly healthy last week and had never, to his knowledge, suffered from heart trouble. . . . This thing will probably be front-page news, not only in France but internationally."

Maigret loathed such cases involving celebrities that had to be handled with kid gloves.

"I'll go," he said.

His report would have to be postponed again. Looking disgruntled, he pushed open the door of the inspectors' room, wondering which of them to take with him. Janvier was there, but he was working on the robbery with assault.

"You go into my room, Janvier, and try to finish my report. . . . You, Lapointe . . ."

Young Lapointe looked up delightedly.

"Put on your hat and come with me."

Then, to Lucas, "If anyone asks for me, I'm at the George V."

"On the poisoning case?"

It had slipped out involuntarily, and Lucas blushed.

"What poisoning case?"

Lucas stammered, "The Countess . . ."

"Who are you talking about?"

"There was something in the reports this morning about a countess with an Italian name who tried to commit suicide at the George V. The reason I didn't tell you . . ."

"Where is the report?"

Lucas rummaged through the papers piled on his desk and pulled out an official sheet of paper.

"She didn't die. . . . That was why . . ."

Maigret scanned the brief statement.

"Has anyone been able to question her?"

"I don't know. Somebody from the Eighteenth Arrondissement went to the Neuilly hospital. I don't know yet whether she was fit to talk. . . ."

Maigret was unaware that shortly before two o'clock that

morning Countess Paverini and Colonel Ward had got out
of a taxi in front of the George V and that it had not surprised the porter to see them pick up their keys together.

Neither had Jules, the room waiter, been surprised when,
answering a summons from number 332, he had found the
Colonel in the Countess's room.

"The usual, Jules!" she had told him.

This meant a bottle of Krug 1947 and a sealed bottle of
Johnny Walker, since the Colonel was suspicious of whisky
that he had not opened himself.

Lucas, who was expecting a lecture, was even more morti-
fied when Maigret just stared at him in surprise, as though
he could not credit such an error of judgment on the part of
his oldest collaborator.

"Come on, Lapointe. . . ."

On the way out they met a petty thief whom Maigret had
sent for.

"Come back and see me this afternoon."

"What time, boss?"

"Whenever you want to."

"Should I get a car?" asked Lapointe.

They got one. Lapointe drove. At the George V, the park-
ing-lot attendant had his orders: "Just leave it here. I'll
park it."

Everyone had their orders. As the two policemen went in,
doors opened before them, and in a few minutes they were
outside suite 347, where the manager was waiting for them.
He had been notified by telephone.

Maigret's job did not often take him to the Hotel George V,
but he had nevertheless been called in there on two or three
occasions, and he knew Monsieur Gilles, with whom he

shook hands. Dr. Frère was waiting in the living room, beside the small table on which his black bag lay. He was a good-looking, composed man whose patients were important people and who knew nearly as many secrets as Maigret himself. But he moved in a different world, one that policemen rarely had the occasion to enter.

"Is he dead?"

A slight flicker of the eyelids.

"About when?"

"Only the post-mortem can establish that accurately, if, as I suppose, there will have to be a post-mortem."

"Could it have been an accident?"

"Come and see."

Maigret did not relish, any more than Monsieur Gilles had, the sight of that naked body in the tub.

"I haven't moved him, since it was useless from a medical point of view. At first sight it might have been one of those accidents that occur in bathtubs more often than you might expect. One slips, and one's head comes up against the rim of the tub. . . ."

"I know. . . . But then there are no marks on the shoulders. Isn't that what you mean?"

Maigret, too, had noticed two darker patches, like bruises, on the dead man's shoulders.

"You believe somebody helped him, don't you?"

"I can't tell. . . . I'd rather let the pathologist decide that question."

"When did you last see him alive?"

"About a week ago, when I came to give the Countess an injection."

18

Monsieur Gilles seemed to scowl. Had he been hoping to keep her out of it?

"A countess with an Italian name?"

"Countess Paverini."

"The one who tried to commit suicide last night?"

"I'm not even sure her attempt was a serious one. She had undoubtedly taken a certain amount of phenobarbital; I knew, actually, that she always took some at night. She took an overdose, but I doubt whether she had swallowed enough to prove fatal."

"A phony suicide?"

"That's what I'm wondering. . . ."

Both of them were familiar with those women—pretty women, almost invariably—who, after a quarrel, a disappointment, some love affair, take just enough sleeping pills to produce the symptoms of poisoning without any real risk to their lives.

"You said the Colonel was present when you gave the Countess her injection?"

"When she was in Paris I used to give her two a week—vitamins B and C, all quite innocuous. Overstrain . . . you understand?"

"And the Colonel?"

Monsieur Gilles took it upon himself to answer.

"The Colonel and the Countess were close friends. They had separate suites—I always wondered why, because . . ."

"He was her lover?"

"The situation was generally accepted—you might say it was official. Two years ago, if I remember correctly, the Colonel asked his wife to divorce him, and everyone in their set expected him to marry the Countess as soon as he was free."

Maigret almost asked, with assumed naïveté: Which set?

What was the use? The telephone rang. Lapointe looked at his boss to find out what he should do. Obviously, the young detective was somewhat overawed by his surroundings.

"Answer it."

"Hello . . . What? . . . Yes, he's here. . . . It's me, yes."

"Who is it?" Maigret asked.

"Lucas wants to talk to you."

"Hello, Lucas . . ."

The latter, to retrieve his previous mistake, had made contact with the American Hospital at Neuilly.

"I'm very sorry, chief. . . . I can't forgive myself. . . . Has she gone back to the hotel?"

Countess Paverini had left her room in the hospital, where she had been alone, and had vanished without anyone trying to stop her.

*In which
we are still concerned
with people whose names recur
constantly in the papers,
and not merely
among the commonplace
local news items*

Just about then an incident occurred that, though apparently insignificant, was to affect Maigret's mood throughout the entire inquiry. Was Lapointe aware of it, or did Maigret attribute to him a reaction that in fact he never had?

A little earlier, when Monsieur Gilles had mentioned the set to which the Countess Paverini and Colonel Ward belonged, the superintendent had restrained himself from asking which set.

If he had done that, wouldn't his voice have betrayed a touch of irritation, of irony, possibly of aggressiveness?

He was reminded of an impression he'd had at the outset of his career on the force. He'd been about Lapointe's age then, and he had been sent, merely to check a statement, into the very district where he was now, between the Etoile and the Seine—he could not remember the name of the street.

At that time, townhouses were still privately owned, and young Maigret had felt he was entering an unfamiliar world. What had struck him most was the quality of its silence, its remoteness from the crowd and the din of traffic. Nothing could be heard but bird song and the rhythmical clatter of horses' hoofs as ladies and gentlemen wearing light-colored derbies rode toward the Bois.

Even the buildings of the area had discreet façades. In the courtyards, one could see chauffeurs polishing the cars, and sometimes, in a doorway or at a window, a valet in a striped waistcoat or a *maître d'hôtel* wearing a white tie.

Then, the young detective knew practically nothing about the private lives of their masters, almost all of whom bore well-known names that could be read any morning in the *Figaro* or the *Gaulois;* and he felt awestruck when he had to ring at one of those majestic doors.

Today, in suite 347, he was certainly no longer the novice he had once been. And by now most of the private mansions had disappeared, and many of the streets that were once so silent had become busy commercial thoroughfares.

Nevertheless, he was at this moment in the district that had formerly housed the aristocracy, and the Hotel George V stood here as the hub of a private universe that was still unfamiliar to him.

The newspapers would publish the names of people who were still asleep or eating their breakfast in neighboring suites. The intersection at Rue François Ier and Avenue Montaigne constituted a world apart, where signs on the houses bore the names of great couturiers, and where even a shirtmaker's shopwindow displayed things to be seen nowhere else.

Wasn't it all rather puzzling for Lapointe, who lived in modest furnished rooms on the Left Bank? Didn't he feel an involuntary respect for this newly revealed luxury, just as Maigret had in the old days?

"A policeman—the ideal policeman—should feel at home in any surroundings."

Maigret had said this one day, and all his life he had striven to forget the surface differences between men, to scrape away the varnish and discover the naked human being under the various appearances.

But this morning he had involuntarily become irritated by something in the atmosphere around him. Monsieur Gilles, the manager, was an excellent person, despite his striped trousers, a certain professional smoothness, and his dread of any sort of trouble; and so was the doctor, with his list of illustrious patients.

He somehow felt a sort of complicity between them. They uttered the same words as everybody else, and yet they spoke a different language. When they mentioned "the Countess" or "the Colonel," the words bore a meaning that eluded ordinary mortals.

In short, they shared a secret. They belonged, if only on the fringe, to a private world toward which the superintendent's conscience would not allow him to display hostility a priori.

No one could tell that this was what he was thinking, or, rather, feeling, as he hung up the receiver and turned to ask the doctor:

"Do you believe that if the Countess really had taken a dose of barbiturates large enough to kill her she would have been able, after your treatment, to get up by herself, about half an hour ago, and leave the hospital?"

"She's gone?"

The bedroom blinds were still closed but those in the living room had been opened, and a little sunshine, just a ray

25

of reflected light, had crept into the room. The doctor was standing next to the table on which his bag was lying. The hotel managér was near the living-room door, and Lapointe a little further back, on Maigret's right.

The dead man was still in the tub, and the bathroom, the door of which stood open, was the most brightly lit of all the rooms.

The telephone rang again. The manager picked up the receiver after a glance at the superintendent, as though to ask his permission.

"Hello, yes? . . . Speaking . . . He's coming up? . . ."

Everyone was staring at him as he stood there looking worried and wondering what to say, when the door to the hall was flung open.

A man of about fifty, tanned and silver-haired, wearing a light-gray suit, looked over the assembled company one by one and finally noticed Monsieur Gilles.

"Ah, there you are. . . . What has happened to David? Where is he? . . ."

"Oh, Mr. Arnold . . ."

He pointed to the bathroom and then, quite naturally, began speaking English.

"How did you hear about it?"

"I called here five times this morning," Arnold replied in the same language.

This was another detail that augmented Maigret's irritation. He could understand English in a pinch, but by no means spoke it fluently. And now the doctor, too, began speaking English.

"Unfortunately, Mr. Arnold, there's no doubt that he is dead."

The newcomer stood in the doorway of the bathroom and stayed there for a while, gazing at the body in the tub with his lips moving as though in silent prayer.

"A stupid accident, I suppose?"

For some unknown reason he had reverted to French, which he spoke with scarcely a trace of an accent.

It was just at that moment that the incident occurred. Maigret was standing beside the chair on which the dead man's trousers had been thrown. There was a slender platinum chain fastened to a button at the waist, to the other end of which, in the pocket, some object such as a key or a watch was presumably attached.

Automatically, out of sheer curiosity, the superintendent reached out to touch the chain, and just as he did so, the man Arnold turned toward him with a severe look, as though to accuse him of unseemly or indelicate behavior.

It was all done much more subtly than by words, with just a glance, barely insistent, and a scarcely perceptible change of expression.

Then Maigret dropped the chain and assumed an attitude of which he promptly felt ashamed, since it was that of a guilty man.

Had Lapointe really noticed this, and averted his eyes on purpose?

There were three of them at police headquarters—it had become a joke—whose admiration for the superintendent amounted to a cult: Lucas, the oldest, Janvier, who had once been as young, as inexperienced, and as enthusiastic as Lapointe, and finally the latter, 'little Lapointe,' as they called him.

Had he been disillusioned, or merely embarrassed, on

seeing his chief affected, just as he was himself, by the atmosphere into which they had suddenly been plunged?

Maigret reacted by stiffening, which was perhaps yet another mistake, as he realized, but he couldn't help it.

"I'd like to ask you a few questions, Monsieur Arnold."

The Englishman did not ask Maigret who he was, but turned toward Monsieur Gilles, who explained:

"Superintendent Maigret of the Department of Criminal Investigation."

He gave a vague and barely courteous little nod.

"May I ask you who you are and why you have come here this morning?"

Once again Arnold looked at the manager in some surprise, as though the question was a peculiar one, to say the least.

"Mr. John Arnold is . . ."

"Let him speak for himself, please."

The Englishman said, "Couldn't we go into the living room?"

Before doing so, he went to cast another glance into the bathroom, as if to pay his respects to the dead man one more time.

"Do you still need me?" asked Dr. Frère.

"As long as I know where to find you . . ."

"My secretary knows where I'll be. . . . The hotel has my phone number."

Arnold asked Monsieur Gilles in English, "Could you have a Scotch sent up for me?"

And Maigret, before resuming the conversation, picked up the receiver.

"Get me the parquet, please, mademoiselle. . . ."

"The what?"

They didn't speak the same language here as at the Quai des Orfèvres.

"Please put me through to the public prosecutor or one of his deputies. . . . Superintendent Maigret . . . Yes. . . ."

While he was waiting, Monsieur Gilles had time to whisper, "Could you ask these gentlemen to act with great discretion, to come into the hotel as if nothing was the matter and . . ."

"Hello! . . . I am at the Hotel George V, *Monsieur le Procureur*. . . . They've just found a man dead in a bathroom, Colonel David Ward. . . . Ward, yes . . . The body is still in the bathtub and there are certain indications that the death was not accidental. . . . Yes . . . So I've been told."

At the other end of the line the public prosecutor had just informed him: "You know that David Ward is a *very important* man?"

Maigret went on listening patiently.

"Yes . . . Yes . . . I'll stay here. . . . There was another incident last night in the same hotel. . . . I'll tell you about that presently. . . . Yes . . . We'll be expecting you. . . ."

While he was speaking, a waiter in a white jacket had appeared briefly and Arnold had sat down in an armchair and lighted a cigar, after slowly and carefully cutting its end.

"I asked you . . ."

"Who I am and what I am doing here . . . Now it's my turn to ask you something: Do you know *who* my friend David Ward is . . . was, as I should say now?"

Perhaps it was not insolence, after all, but innate self-assurance. Arnold was at home here. The manager was reluctant to interrupt him but eventually did so, rather like a

29

schoolboy asking leave to go to the washroom during a lesson.

"Will you excuse me, gentlemen. I'd like to know whether I may go downstairs to give certain instructions."

"We are expecting the department of public prosecution."

"Yes, so I gathered."

"We shall need you. I am also expecting some technical experts and photographers, as well as the police pathologist."

"May I ask that at least some of these gentlemen come in through the service entrance? You must understand, superintendent. If there is too much coming and going in the front lobby and if . . ."

"I understand."

"Thank you. Your whisky will be up any minute, Mr. Arnold. May I offer you something, gentlemen?"

Maigret shook his head and then regretted it, for he could have used a drink himself.

"I'm listening, Monsieur Arnold. You were saying?"

"I was saying that you have probably read my friend David's name in the papers like everyone else . . . generally accompanied by the word 'multimillionaire' . . . 'the English multimillionaire.' And that's quite true, if you reckon in francs, though not in pounds."

"How old was he?" cut in Maigret.

"Sixty-three. David did not make his fortune himself but, as we say, he was born with a silver spoon in his mouth. His father already owned the biggest wire mills in Manchester, founded by his grandfather. Are you following me?"

"I'm following you."

"I won't go so far as to say that the business ran itself

and that David didn't have to bother about it, but it required very little effort from him, an occasional interview with his directors, a board meeting, some documents to sign."

"He didn't live in Manchester?"

"Hardly ever."

"According to the newspapers . . ."

"The newspapers adopt two or three dozen public figures, once and for all, and detail their most trivial activities. That does not mean that everything they say is accurate. Thus with regard to David's divorces they printed a great many unfounded stories. . . . But that's not what I want to try and make you understand. . . . In most people's view, David, who had inherited a considerable fortune and a sound business, had nothing to do but enjoy himself in Paris, at Deauville, Cannes, Lausanne, or in Rome, frequenting night clubs and race courses in the company of pretty women and other well-known public figures. But that is not the case. . . ."

Arnold took his time, stared for a moment at the white ash of his cigar, then beckoned to the waiter who had just come in, and took his glass of whisky from the tray.

"If you don't mind . . ."

Then, sinking back into his armchair:

"If David never led the usual life of a rich British industrialist in Manchester, it was just because his position there was already established and he had nothing to do but carry on the work of his father and his grandfather, which did not interest him at all. Can you understand that?"

And from the way he looked at the superintendent and then at young Lapointe, it was clear that he considered the two men incapable of understanding such a feeling.

"The Americans have a word which we in England don't

use very often. . . . They speak of a 'playboy,' meaning a rich man whose sole aim in life is to have a good time, playing polo or going skiing, yacht racing, frequenting night clubs in pleasant company. . . ."

"The men from the public prosecutor's office will soon be here," observed Maigret, looking at his watch.

"I apologize for inflicting this lecture on you, but you asked me a question which I cannot answer in a couple of words. Perhaps, too, I'm anxious to save you from making blunders . . . *gaffes,* I think you say. Far from being a playboy, David Ward took a personal interest, not merely in his capacity as owner of the Ward Wire Mills of Manchester, but in a number of widely differing concerns as well. Only he did not consider it necessary to shut himself up eight hours a day in an office in order to work. Believe me when I tell you he was a businessman of genius. . . . He used to bring off remarkable deals at the most unexpected times and places . . ."

"For instance?"

"Once when we were driving together on the Italian Riviera, some trouble with his Rolls obliged us to stop at a modest little inn. While our meal was being prepared David and I went for a walk in the neighborhood. This was about twenty years ago. By that same evening we were in Rome, but a few days later I had to buy on David's behalf five thousand acres of land, partly covered with vineyards. Today you would find there three grand hotels, a casino, and one of the prettiest stretches of beach along the coast laid out with villas. . . . While in Switzerland, near Montreux . . ."

"In short, you were his personal business agent?"

"His friend and his business agent, if you like. His friend

32

primarily, for when I first knew him I had never had anything to do with commerce or finance."

"Are you staying at the George V, too?"

"No, at the Hotel Scribe. It may seem odd to you, but in Paris as elsewhere we almost always lived in separate hotels, for David always guarded his privacy most jealously."

"Was it for the same reason that Countess Paverini stayed in a suite at the farther end of the corridor?"

Arnold reddened slightly.

"For that reason among others."

"Meaning . . . ?"

"It was a question of discretion."

"But didn't everybody know about their relationship?"

"Everybody talked about it, certainly."

"And was it true?"

"I suppose so. I never asked him any questions on that subject."

"And yet you were intimate friends . . ."

Now it was Arnold's turn to be annoyed. He, too, must be thinking that they were not speaking the same language, that they were on different wave lengths.

"How many legal wives has he had?"

"Only three. The newspapers have ascribed more to him because whenever he met a woman and was seen in public with her a few times there were rumors of another marriage."

"Are the three wives still living?"

"Yes."

"Did he have any children by them?"

"Two. A son, Bobby, who's eighteen and is at Cambridge, by the second, and a daughter, Ellen, by the third."

"On what kind of terms was he with them?"

"With his former wives? On excellent terms. He was a gentleman."

"Did he sometimes see them?"

"He met them occasionally. . . ."

"Are they wealthy?"

"Only the first, Dorothy Payne, whose people own an important textile firm in Manchester."

"What about the other two?"

"He has provided for them."

"So that none of them had anything to gain by his death?"

Arnold gave a puzzled frown and looked shocked.

"Why should they?"

"And Countess Paverini?"

"He would no doubt have married her once his divorce from Muriel Halligan had been made final."

"In your opinion, who had something to gain by his death?"

The answer was swift and unhesitating: "Nobody."

"Did he have any enemies, to your knowledge?"

"Only friends, as far as I know."

"Had he come to the George V for a long stay?"

"Wait a minute. . . . This is the seventh of October. . . ."

He took out his diary, a pretty little book bound in soft red leather with gilt edges.

"We arrived from Cannes on the second. . . . Before that we were in Biarritz, having left Deauville on August 17. . . . We were to leave for Lausanne on the thirteenth. . . ."

"On business?"

Once again Arnold cast a despairing glance, as though this thick-skulled man was hopelessly incapable of understanding the most elementary things.

"David had an apartment at Lausanne, and has even made his home there."

"And here?"

"He has this suite, which he rents by the year, as he does one in London and another at the Carlton in Cannes. . . ."

"And in Manchester?"

"He owns the Ward family mansion, an enormous Victorian structure, where I don't suppose he's spent three nights in the last thirty years. . . . He detested Manchester."

"Do you know Countess Paverini well?"

Arnold did not have time to answer. Footsteps and voices were echoing in the corridor. Monsieur Gilles, obviously more impressed than he had been by Maigret, ushered in the public prosecutor and a young examining magistrate with whom the superintendent had not previously worked; his name was Calas and he looked like a student.

"This is Mr. Arnold."

"I am John Arnold," he introduced himself.

Maigret went on: "The close friend and personal business agent of the deceased."

Seemingly delighted to be dealing with someone important at last, Arnold turned to the public prosecutor:

"I had arranged a rendezvous with David for ten o'clock this morning—to be accurate, I was to ring him up. That was how I heard of his death. I now learn that it is thought not to have been an accident, and I suppose the police have good reasons for saying so. What I would like to ask you, *Monsieur le Procureur,* is to avoid too much talk getting around about the affair. David was an important man and I cannot tell you how many repercussions his death will involve, not only on the stock exchange but in various other circles."

"We shall be as discreet as possible," murmured the public prosecutor. "Don't you agree, superintendent?"

Maigret nodded.

"I suppose," Arnold went on, "that you have questions to put to me?"

The public prosecutor looked at Maigret, then at the examining magistrate.

"Presently, perhaps . . . I don't know. . . . For the time being, I think that you are free to . . ."

"If you need me, I shall be downstairs. . . . In the bar . . ."

When the door had closed behind Arnold, Maigret and the prosecutor exchanged worried looks.

"A grotesque incident, isn't it?" said the public prosecutor. "Do you have any ideas?"

"Not a single one. Except that a certain Countess Paverini, who was Ward's mistress and who lived in a suite at the far end of the hall, tried to poison herself last night. The doctor had her taken to the American Hospital at Neuilly, where she was given a private room. The nurse went to visit her every half hour. A little while ago she found the room empty."

"The countess has vanished?"

Maigret nodded, and went on: "I've had a watch put on the stations, the airports, and all the other routes out of Paris."

"It's strange, isn't it?"

Maigret shrugged his shoulders. What could he say? Everything about this case was strange, from the dead man who had been born with a silver spoon in his mouth and who carried on business while frequenting race tracks and night clubs, to that socialite man of affairs who had talked to him as a schoolmaster would address a dull pupil.

"Do you want to see him?"

The public prosecutor, a highly dignified magistrate who belonged to the old aristocracy of the legal profession, confessed:

"I called the Ministry of Foreign Affairs. . . . David Ward really was an important person. He acquired his Colonel's rank during the war, as head of a branch of Intelligence. . . . Do you think that might have something to do with his death?"

Footsteps sounded in the corridor, followed by a knock on the door, and Dr. Paul appeared, carrying his bag.

"I actually thought they were going to make me use the service entrance. That's what's happening downstairs to your technical people. . . . Where's the body?"

He shook hands with the prosecutor, with Calas, the new magistrate, and finally with Maigret.

"Well, my old partner?"

Then he took off his jacket and rolled up his shirt sleeves.

"A man or a woman?"

"A man."

Maigret showed the doctor the bathroom, and they heard him utter an exclamation. The men from the technical branch arrived next, bringing their apparatus, and Maigret had to oversee them.

At the Hotel George V, just as anywhere else, and for David Ward, just as for any other victim of a crime, routine had to be followed.

"Can we open the blinds, Chief?"

37

"Yes. This glass doesn't count; it was just brought up for a witness."

By now the sun was flooding the living room and also the bedroom, a large, bright room containing, as they now discovered, quantities of small personal possessions, almost all rare or precious objects.

For instance, the alarm clock on the bedside table was gold and came from Cartier, as did a cigar case lying on a chest of drawers, while the manicure set bore the mark of a famous London firm.

In the wardrobe an inspector counted eighteen suits, and there were probably as many in Ward's other homes, at Cannes, at Lausanne, in London.

"You can send in the photographer," said Dr. Paul's voice.

Maigret looked around, at nothing in particular, taking in the smallest details of the apartment and what was in it.

"Will you call Lucas and find out if he has any news," he told Lapointe, who seemed a bit bewildered by the general hubbub.

There were three telephones, one in the living room, a second at the head of the bed, and the third in the bathroom.

"Hello, Lucas? . . . Lapointe speaking. . . ."

By the window, Maigret was talking in an undertone to the prosecutor and the examining magistrate, while Dr. Paul and the photographer were still out of sight in the bathroom.

"We'll see whether Dr. Paul confirms Dr. Frère's opinion. According to him, the bruises . . ."

The police doctor re-emerged at last, as cheerful as usual.

"Pending my report and probably the post-mortem—I assume one will be ordered—I can tell you this:

"First, that guy was built to last to at least eighty.

"Second, he was pretty drunk when he got into his bath.

"Third, he didn't slip, and the person who helped him meet his end had to use a certain amount of force to hold him under the water.

"That's all for the moment. If you'll have him sent to the Forensic Laboratory for me I'll try to find out more...."

The two magistrates exchanged a glance. Post-mortem or no post-mortem?

"Does he have any relatives?" the prosecutor asked Maigret.

"From what I could find out he has two children, both minors, and the divorce proceedings from his third wife haven't been completed yet."

"Brothers or sisters?"

"Just a minute..."

Maigret picked up the phone again. Lapointe was signaling that he wanted to talk to him, but the superintendent had already asked for the bar.

"Mr. Arnold, please."

"Just a minute..."

Shortly after that, Maigret informed the magistrate:

"No sister. He had a brother who was killed in India at the age of twenty-two. He has some cousins with whom he has lost contact. What did you want to say, Lapointe?"

"Lucas told me one detail he has just uncovered. This morning, about nine o'clock, Countess Paverini made several telephone calls from her bedroom."

"Did they record the numbers?"

"Not the Paris calls; there were two or three of those, and she called one number twice. Then she called Monte Carlo . . ."

"What number?"

"The Hotel de Paris."

"To speak to whom?"

"They don't know. Would you like me to call the Hotel de Paris?"

The milieu was still the same: in Paris, the George V, and at Monte Carlo, the most sumptuous hotel on the Riviera.

"Hello, mademoiselle, will you please get me the Hotel de Paris, Monte Carlo? . . . What did you say?"

He turned to the superintendent in some embarrassment.

"She's asking to whose account the call should be charged."

And Maigret replied impatiently: "To Ward's . . . Or to mine, if she'd rather . . ."

"Hello, mademoiselle . . . The call is for Superintendent Maigret. . . . Yes . . . Thank you."

He hung up and reported that there would be a ten-minute wait.

In one drawer, some letters had been found, some in English, others in French or Italian, letters from women amidst business correspondence, invitations to cocktail parties and dinners; in another drawer were neatly classified files.

"Should we take them?"

Maigret nodded, after a questioning glance at Calas, the examining magistrate.

It was eleven o'clock and the hotel was beginning to come

to life. They could hear bells ringing, servants coming and going, and the continuous click of the elevator.

"Doctor, do you think a woman could have held his head under the water?"

"That depends on the woman."

"They call her the 'little Countess,' which suggests that she's of slight build."

"It's not size or weight that count," muttered Dr. Paul philosophically.

And Maigret added: "Maybe we should go have a look at 332."

"What's 332?"

"It's that countess's suite."

The door was locked and they had to find a maid. The suite had already been cleaned; it, too, consisted of a living room, smaller than the one in 347, a bedroom, and a bathroom.

Although the window was open, the air was still redolent of perfume and alcohol, and while the bottle of champagne had been removed, the whisky bottle, three quarters full, still stood on a small table.

The public prosecutor and the examining magistrate, too well brought up or too timid, stood hesitating on the threshold while Maigret flung open closets and drawers. What he discovered was the feminine equivalent of what he had found in Ward's rooms: luxury articles available only in very exclusive shops, the symbols of a certain life style.

Jewels were scattered around on the dressing table as if they were worthless baubles: a diamond bracelet, a tiny watch, earrings and rings worth some twenty million francs all told.

Here, too, there were papers in a drawer, invitations, dressmakers' and milliners' bills, prospectuses, timetables from Air France and Pan American.

There were no personal letters, as though the little Countess neither wrote nor received any. On the other hand, in a closet Maigret counted twenty-eight pairs of shoes, some of which had never been worn; their size implied that the Countess was indeed a tiny person.

Lapointe rushed in.

"I just got through to the Hotel de Paris. The operator logs outgoing but not incoming calls, except when guests are out and she has to leave a message for them. She's had more than fifteen calls from Paris this morning and can't say who this one was for."

Lapointe added hesitantly: "She asked me if it's as hot here as it is down there. Apparently . . ."

No one was listening to him now, and he stopped talking. The little group went back to David Ward's suite and met a somewhat odd procession. The manager, who had undoubtedly been summoned, walked in front, like a scout, anxiously watching in case any door should open suddenly. He had enlisted one of the bellboys in sky-blue uniform as a reinforcement to run interference for them.

Four men followed, carrying on a stretcher the still-naked body of David Ward concealed under a blanket.

"This way," Monsieur Gilles said in a muffled voice.

He was walking on tiptoe. The bearers moved forward cautiously, trying to steer clear of walls and doors.

They didn't go toward any of the main elevators, but took a narrow, dingily painted hall that led to the freight elevator.

David Ward, who had been one of the most distinguished

of the hotel's guests, was leaving it by the back way, the one used for trunks and heavy baggage.

There was a silence. The magistrates, who had nothing else to do, were reluctant to return to the suite.

"You take care of things, Maigret," sighed the public prosecutor.

He hesitated, then, lowering his voice: "Be discreet. Try to stop the press . . . well, you know what I mean . . . The Ministry has strongly suggested . . ."

Things had been less complicated yesterday at about the same time, when the superintendent had visited the cashier on Rue de Clignancourt, the father of three children, who had received two bullet wounds in the stomach while trying to protect his wallet, which contained eight million francs.

He had refused to be taken to a hospital. If he was going to die, he wanted to do so in the little room with the pink-flowered wallpaper where his wife was nursing him and where his children, home from school, walked around on tiptoe.

There was a clue in that case, the beret that had been dropped on the spot, which would eventually put him on the track of the criminals.

But the case of David Ward?

"I think," Maigret said suddenly, as though talking to himself, "that I'll take a trip to Orly."

Maybe because of the Air France and Pan Am schedules that were lying around in a drawer, or the phone call to Monte Carlo?

Maybe, after all, because he had to do something and an airport seemed to fit in with a person like the little Countess.

43

*Which tells
of the little Countess's
comings and goings,
and of Maigret's
scruples*

He couldn't get away from the George V as soon as he had
hoped. Before leaving for the airport, while Maigret was giving instructions over the telephone to Lucas, young Lapointe,
who had been prowling around Countess Paverini's suite,
came up with a colored tin box; it had originally contained
English cookies—now it was full of photographs.

It reminded Maigret of the box in which, when he was
small, his mother used to keep buttons, and from which she
would fish one out whenever a garment was missing one.
That tin had been a teabox decorated with Chinese charac-
ters, a somewhat unexpected object to find in the home of a
country-estate manager who never drank tea.

In a closet in suite 332, the superintendent had noticed
suitcases from a celebrated trunkmaker's on Avenue
Marceau, and the most trivial common articles—a shoehorn or a paper weight—bearing the imprints of luxury
firms.

Yet it was in an ordinary cookie tin that the Countess
kept, jumbled together, photographs of herself and her
friends, snapshots taken in the various places she had

stayed, showing her in a bathing suit on a yacht, probably in the Mediterranean, or water-skiing, or enjoying winter sports on a snowy mountain slope. On a number of these photographs she appeared with the Colonel, sometimes alone with him, more frequently with other people whom the superintendent happened to recognize, since they were actors and writers, people whose pictures were often in the newspapers.

"Are you taking the tin, sir?"

Maigret seemed strangely loath to leave that floor of the George V, although there was really nothing more for him to find there.

"Get the nurse. First make sure it's the same one who was on duty last night."

It was the same one, for the simple reason that there weren't any others on the hotel staff. Her work consisted chiefly, as Maigret soon found out, of relieving hangovers and giving injections. For the last few years, one third of the guests had been receiving injections of some kind or other on their doctors' orders.

"Tell me, Mademoiselle . . ."

" . . . Genévrier . . ."

She was a dignified, sad-looking person of indeterminate age, with the glazed eyes of someone who never gets enough sleep.

"When Countess Paverini left the hotel in the ambulance, she was in her nightgown, wasn't she?"

"Yes. We wrapped a blanket around her. I didn't want to waste time dressing her. I put some clothes for her in a suitcase."

"A dress?"

46

"A blue suit, the first thing I could lay my hands on. Shoes and stockings, too, of course."

"Nothing else?"

"A purse that was lying around the room. I made sure it contained a comb, compact, lipstick, all the things a woman needs."

"Do you know whether there was any money in the bag?"

"I saw a billfold, a checkbook, and a passport. . . ."

"A French passport?"

"An Italian one."

"Is the Countess Italian by birth?"

"She's French. She became Italian by her marriage to Count Paverini and I think she's kept that nationality. I don't know. That's none of my business."

In the elevator there was a man at whom Lapointe stared avidly and whom Maigret eventually recognized as the greatest comedian in American movies. He, too, found it odd, after seeing him so often on the screen, to meet him in the flesh in a hotel elevator, dressed like anyone else, with bags under his eyes and the depressed expression of a man who has drunk too much the night before.

On his way to the reception area, the superintendent walked through the bar, where John Arnold was standing at the counter with a glass of whisky in front of him.

"Will you come over here for a minute?"

There were only a few customers there, most of them looking as bilious as the American actor, except for one couple who had spread out business papers on a small table and were deep in serious discussion.

Maigret handed the photographs, one by one, to his companion.

"I suppose you know all these people? I noticed you were on some of the snapshots. . . ."

Arnold did in fact know them all, and many of them were people whose names Maigret himself knew: two former kings who had once reigned in their own countries and were now living on the Riviera, an ex-queen who lived at Lausanne, a few princes, an English theatrical producer, the proprietor of a leading brand of whisky, a ballerina, and a tennis champion.

There was something irritating about the way Arnold referred to them.

"You don't recognize him? That's Paul."

"Paul what?"

"Paul of Yugoslavia. And there's Nenette."

Nenette was not the name of a starlet or a demimondaine, but that of a lady of the Faubourg Saint-Germain, an aristocratic hostess who entertained ministers and ambassadors.

"And who's this with the Countess and the Colonel?"

"Jef."

"Jef what?"

"Jef Van Meulen, of the chemical products firm."

Another name that Maigret knew, of course, having seen it on cans of paint and a host of other products.

Jef was wearing shorts and a huge straw sombrero, and he was bowling in one of the squares of Saint-Tropez.

"He was the Countess's second husband."

"One more question, Mr. Arnold. Do you know anyone presently living at the Hotel de Paris in Monte Carlo whom the Countess would call if she was in trouble?"

"Did she ring up Monte Carlo?"

"I asked you a question."

"Jef, of course."

"You mean her second husband?"

"He spends a good part of the year on the Riviera. He owns a villa at Mougins, near Cannes, but most of the time he prefers the Hotel de Paris."

"Are they still on good terms?"

"Excellent. She always calls him Daddy."

The American comedian, after taking a stroll around the lobby, had come up to lean against the bar, and without asking what he wanted the bartender automatically mixed him a large glass of gin and tomato juice.

"Were Van Meulen and the Colonel on good terms?"

"They were very old friends."

"And Count Paverini?"

"He's on one of the photographs you've just shown me."

Arnold picked it out. A tall, dark young man with a fine head of hair, in bathing trunks, at the prow of a yacht.

"Another friend?"

"Why not?"

"Thanks a lot . . ."

Maigret was about to leave, then changed his mind.

"Do you know who the Colonel's lawyer is?"

Once again Arnold betrayed some impatience, as though his interlocutor was really excessively ignorant.

"He had a great many. Not necessarily the sort of lawyer you would call a *notaire* in France. In London he had a firm of solicitors called Philps, Philps and Hadley; in New York, Harrison and Shaw looked after his interests; in Lausanne . . ."

"And to which of these firms do you think he has entrusted his will?"

"He left wills all over the place. He was always changing them."

Maigret had accepted the whisky he had been offered, but Lapointe, out of tact, merely took a glass of beer.

"Thank you, Mr. Arnold."

"Above all, don't forget what I have told you. Be careful. You'll see, there'll be trouble."

Maigret was so convinced of that that he wore his darkest look. He was annoyed by all these people whose habits were so different from those of ordinary mortals. He realized that he was ill equipped to understand them and that it would take him months to become familiar with their ways.

"Come on, Lapointe."

He hurried through the lobby without looking right or left, for fear of being buttonholed by Monsieur Gilles, whom he found pleasant enough but from whom he would inevitably get another lecture on prudence and discretion. By now the lobby was almost full of people speaking every conceivable language and smoking cigarettes and cigars from every country under the sun.

"This way, Monsieur Maigret . . ."

The car attendant led him to the spot where he had parked the small police car between a Rolls and a Cadillac.

To tip or not to tip? Maigret did not tip him.

"To Orly, son . . ."

"Yes, Chief . . ."

The superintendent would have liked to go to the American Hospital at Neuilly to interrogate the nurse, the receptionist, the switchboard operator. There were millions of things he would have liked to do and should have done. But he couldn't be everywhere at once, and he was anxious to meet the little Countess, as her friends called her.

She was indeed a little person, slight and pretty, as he knew from her photographs. How old would she be? It was hard to tell from the pictures, most of them taken in bright sunlight, which showed more of her body, half-naked in a bikini, than of any facial details.

She was dark, with a pert, pointed little nose, bright eyes, and a propensity for *gamine* poses.

He could have sworn, though, that she was pushing forty. The hotel register would have told him, but it hadn't occurred to him in time. He was working on the most pressing matters first, with the disagreeable feeling that he was sabotaging his own investigation.

"You'll have to go back to the George V pretty soon," he told Lapointe, "to look at her registration form. Get the clearest picture enlarged."

"Should we send it to the papers?"

"Not yet. Then go to the American Hospital. Got it?"

"Yes. Are you leaving?"

That wasn't certain but he could feel it coming.

"Anyway, if I do go, give my wife a call."

He had flown four or five times, but that was a while back, and he barely recognized Orly. New buildings had shot up, and there was now more traffic here than at the Gare du Nord or the Gare Saint-Lazare.

Unlike the train stations, at the airport, just as at the George V, one heard every language being spoken and saw tips being given in every variety of currency. Newspaper photographers, swarming over a large car, were taking pictures of a celebrity whose arms were full of flowers and

whose suitcases were the same famous brand as those of the
little Countess.

"Should I wait for you, Chief?"

"No. Drive downtown and do what I said. If I don't leave
I'll take a cab."

He skipped through the crowd to dodge the journalists,
and by the time he had reached the main hall, where the
desks of the various airlines stood in a row, two cameras had
been set up, while a group of Hindus, some in turbans,
crossed the hall and headed for the customs office.

The loud-speaker emitted continuous calls.

"Calling Mr. Stilwell . . . Mr. Stilwell . . . Would Mr. Stilwell please report to the Pan American ticket office. . . ."

The request was repeated in English; then came another
in Spanish, asking for Señorita Consuelo Gonzales.

The office of the special airport superintendent was no
longer where it used to be; Maigret finally found it, however, and pushed open the door.

"Hello, Colombani . . ."

Colombani, whose wedding Maigret had attended, was
not with the crime squad, but was directly responsible to the
Ministry of the Interior.

"Was it you who sent me the note?"

Superintendent Colombani was hunting through his dis-
organized desk for a scrap of paper on which the name of
the Countess had been scribbled in pencil.

"You haven't seen her?"

"I gave the word to the inspectors. . . . I haven't heard anything yet. . . . I'll check the passenger lists. . . ."

He went into another office with a glass door, and came
back with a bunch of papers.

"Just a minute . . . Flight 315 for London . . . Paverini . . . Paverini . . . No . . . There's no Paverini among the passengers. . . . You don't know where she was going? . . . The next plane: Stuttgart . . . No Paverini here either . . . Cairo, Beirut . . . P . . . Potteret . . . No! . . . New York by Pan Am . . . Pittsberg . . . Piroulet . . . Still no Paverini . . ."

"Have there been any flights to the Riviera?"

"The Rome plane, stopping over at Nice, yes, at ten thirty-two."

"Do you have the passenger list?"

"I have the list of passengers for Rome, because my men checked their passports. . . . They don't worry about passengers to Nice, who go in by a different gate and don't have to go through customs and police formalities. . . ."

"Is it a French plane?"

"A British one . . . Come and see B.E.A. . . . I'll take you there."

In the entrance hall the counters were lined up like fairground booths, crowned with panels bearing the colors of different countries, usually with mysterious initials.

"Do you have the passenger list for flight 312?"

The attendant, an English girl with a freckled face, looked through her files and held out a sheet.

"P . . . P . . . Pearson . . . Paverini, Louise, Countess Paverini . . . Is that it, Maigret?"

Maigret addressed the English girl.

"Can you tell me if this passenger had reserved her seat?"

"Just a minute . . . My colleague was on duty at the time. . . ."

She left her desk, plunged into the crowd, and finally returned with a tall, fair-haired young man who spoke French with a strong English accent.

"Were you the one who made out a ticket for Countess Paverini?"

He replied in the affirmative. His neighbor from Alitalia had brought her over. She was determined to get to Nice and had missed the Air France plane that morning.

"It's complicated, you know. There are some planes that fly on certain lines only once or twice a week. The stops are not always the same on some routes. I told her that if we had a vacancy at the last minute . . ."

"Did she take the plane?"

"Yes, at ten twenty-eight."

"So she's already arrived in Nice?"

The employee looked up at a clock on the opposite wall.

"Half an hour ago."

"How did she pay for her ticket?"

"By check. She explained to me that she had left in a hurry and didn't have any cash on her."

"Do you usually accept checks?"

"When the travelers are well-known people."

"Have you still got hers?"

He opened a drawer, flipped through a few papers, and extracted a sheet to which a pale-blue check was clipped. The check was drawn, not on a French bank, but on a Swiss bank that had a branch on Avenue de l'Opéra. The writing was a feverish, irregular scrawl.

"Thank you."

And, to Colombani: "Can I call Nice from your office?"

"You may even send a message by Telex that will be received immediately."

"I'd rather talk to them."

"Come with me. . . . Is it something important?"

"Very!"

"Tough case?"

"I'm afraid so."

"Is it the airport police you want to talk to?"

Maigret nodded.

"It'll take a few minutes. We have time for a drink. . . . This way . . . Will you let us know when you get through to Nice, Dutilleul?"

At the bar they squeezed in between a Brazilian family and some pilots in gray uniforms speaking French with a Swiss or Belgian accent.

"What'll you have?"

"I just had a whisky. I'd better stick with that."

Colombani explained: "The message we had from police headquarters didn't mention passengers for a French airport. Since we only deal, as a rule, with those who have to get their passports visaed . . ."

Maigret drained his glass because he had just been summoned to the phone.

"Hello . . . Is this the airport police? . . . Maigret speaking, Department of Criminal Investigation . . . Yes . . . Can you hear me? . . . Hello, I'm speaking as clearly as I can . . . A young woman . . . Hello! Countess Paverini . . . *P* as in Peter, *a* as in apple, *v* as in Victor, *e* as in Edward, *rini,* yes . . . She must have left on a B.E.A. plane a little over half an hour ago. . . . Yes, the plane from London via Paris . . . What? I can't hear a thing. . . ."

Considerately Colombani went to close the door because the din from the airport, including the sound of a plane approaching the huge glass doors, pervaded the office.

"The plane has just landed? A delay, what? All the better . . . Are the passengers still in the airport? . . . Hello! . . . Go as fast as you can. . . . Paverini . . . No . . . Detain her under some pretext or other . . . to check her papers, for instance. Hurry."

Colombani commented knowingly, "I thought there'd be a delay. There are storm warnings all along the route. The Casablanca plane was an hour and a half late and the . . ."

"Hello! . . . Yes . . . What? . . . You saw her? . . . So, what? . . . She's gone?"

At the other end of the line, too, the noise of an engine could be heard.

"Is that the plane leaving? . . . Is she on board? . . . No?"

He eventually understood that the policeman had just missed her. The passengers from London were still there, since they had to go through customs, but the Countess, who had boarded in Paris, had left first and immediately got into a waiting car.

"A car with a Belgian license plate, you said? . . . Yes, I hear you; a big car . . . chauffeur-driven . . . No . . . Nothing . . . Thank you . . ."

From the American Hospital she had telephoned Monte Carlo, where her second husband, Joseph Van Meulen, was probably staying at the Hotel de Paris. Then she'd had herself driven to Orly and had taken the first plane to the Riviera. At Nice a big Belgian car was waiting for her.

"Are things working out all right?" queried Colombani.

"What time is there a plane for Nice?"

"At one nineteen . . . As a rule they're full, even though

it's the off-season. . . . But at the last minute there are always one or two passengers who don't show up. . . . Would you like me to book you a seat?"

Without Colombani, Maigret would have lost precious time.

"That's done. Now you only have to wait. They'll send for you when the time comes. Will you be in the restaurant?"

Maigret lunched alone in a corner after phoning Lucas, who had nothing new to tell him.

"The journalists aren't on to it yet?"

"I don't think so. I saw one prowling around the corridor just now, but it was Michaux, who's always hanging around the place, and he didn't say anything to me. . . ."

"Lapointe knows what to do. . . . I'll call back from Nice during the afternoon. . . ."

They came and got Maigret, as promised, and he followed the line of passengers to the aircraft, where he took a seat at the back. He had left the tin of photographs with Lapointe, but had kept a few of them that seemed to him the most interesting; and instead of reading the newspaper the stewardess offered him with a pack of chewing gum, he began to examine them thoughtfully.

He had to wait to smoke his pipe and unfasten his seat belt until the lighted warning in front of him went out; then almost immediately he was offered tea and cakes, which he did not want.

Reclining in his armchair with his eyes half-closed, he seemed to be thinking of nothing as the aircraft flew over a thick carpet of luminous clouds. Actually he was trying to bring to life names and figures that only that morning had been as unfamiliar to him as the inhabitants of another planet.

How long would it be before the death of the Colonel became known and the press got hold of the affair? That was when complications would begin, as they always do when a public figure is involved. Wouldn't the London papers send reporters to Paris? According to John Arnold, David Ward had interests in most parts of the world. What a strange man he was! Maigret had only seen him in a pitiful and grotesque position, naked in his bath, with a big pallid paunch emerging as though it were floating.

Had Lapointe felt that at a certain point the superintendent had been taken aback, had not been quite equal to his task; had his faith in his chief been shaken?

It was a fact that these people exasperated him. Confronting them, he was in the situation of a new member of some club, or a new boy at school, who feels awkward and ashamed because he does not yet know the rules, the customs, the passwords, and who imagines that the others are laughing at him.

He was convinced that John Arnold, so easy and self-confident in the company of bankers and ex-kings in London, Rome, Berlin, or New York, had been amused by his gaucherie and had treated him with a somewhat pitying condescension.

Maigret, just as everyone else, knew, and better than most people because of his job, how certain kinds of business are handled, how certain sets of people live. But his knowledge was theoretical. He didn't have a feel for it. Tiny details puzzled him.

This was the first time he had had anything to do with

that privileged society, news of which as a rule reaches one only through the indiscretions of the press.

There are some multimillionaires, to use the accepted term, who are easily identified and whose way of life can be more or less imagined, big businessmen or bankers who go to their offices every day and who in their private lives are not so very different from the rest of humanity.

He had known some important industrialists in northern and eastern France, wool merchants or iron magnates, who were at work by eight in the morning and in bed by ten at night, whose family life was not unlike those of their managers and foremen.

He had begun to realize now that these men were not exactly at the top of the ladder, that they were small fry compared to the really rich.

Above them were men like Colonel Ward, and perhaps like Joseph Van Meulen, who practically never set foot in an office now but went from one grand hotel to another, surrounded by pretty women, cruising on their yachts, cultivating complicated interrelationships, and meeting in hotel lounges or night clubs to handle business matters far more important than those of the middle-class financiers.

David Ward had had three legal wives, whose names Maigret had put down in his notebook. Dorothy Payne, the first, was the only one who had belonged to more or less the same social set and was, like Ward himself, a native of Manchester. They had had no children and had divorced after three years. She had since remarried.

However, she had not reverted to the bourgeois world of her family after her divorce, and she had not gone back to Manchester. She had married a replica of Ward, so to speak, an Italian artificial-silk magnate named Aldo de Rocca who had a passion for motor cars and raced at Le Mans every year.

Presumably he, too, stayed at the George V or the Ritz in Paris, at the Savoy in London, at the Carlton in Cannes, at the Hotel de Paris in Monte Carlo.

All these people must inevitably have met constantly. There are only some twenty or thirty real luxury hotels in the world, a dozen or so fashionable seaside resorts, a limited number of social occasions, Ascots and Grand Prix race meetings. Everyone patronizes the same dressmakers, tailors and jewelers, the same hairdressers and manicurists.

The Colonel's second wife, Alice Perrin, whose son was at Cambridge, came from a different milieu, being the daughter of a village schoolteacher in Nièvre, and had been working as a fashion model when Ward met her.

But fashion models, too, live on the fringes of the same world.

On her divorce she had not resumed her profession, but the Colonel had provided her with an income.

What sort of people did she frequent now?

The same question could have been asked about the third, Muriel Halligan, daughter of an overseer in Hoboken, who had been selling cigarettes in a Broadway night club when David Ward fell in love with her.

She lived in Lausanne now with her daughter, and she, too, was free of financial anxieties.

Was John Arnold married, incidentally? Maigret could have wagered he was not. He seemed born to be factotum, the eminent sage, and confidant to a man like Ward. He must belong to a good English family, possibly a very old family having come down in the world. He had probably been to Eton and Cambridge, gone out for golf, tennis, rowing, and sailing. No doubt before meeting Ward he had been in the army or in the foreign service.

The fact remained that he had led, in the Colonel's shadow, the sort of life he seemed made for. Who knows? Perhaps he discreetly took advantage not only of his patron's love of luxury but of his love affairs.

"Ladies and gentlemen, kindly fasten your seat belts and refrain from smoking. In a few minutes we shall be landing at Nice. We hope you have had a pleasant journey. . . ."

Maigret had some difficulty emptying his pipe into the minute ashtray embedded in the arm of his chair, and his broad fingers struggled with the buckle of his belt. He had not noticed that for the last few moments they had been flying over the sea, which suddenly came up quite close to the porthole, almost vertically, as the plane began to swing around; there were some fishing boats that looked like toys and a two-masted sailing ship that left a silvery wake behind it.

"Kindly remain in your seats until the aircraft comes to a complete stop. . . ."

The plane touched the ground, bounced slightly, and the engine grew noisier as it approached the white building of the airport. Maigret's ears were buzzing.

He was one of the last to deplane because he was far to the rear and a stout lady in front of him had left a box of chocolates in her seat and was struggling back against the stream.

At the foot of the gangway a young man wearing no jacket, his shirt gleaming in the sunshine, spoke to him and raised a finger to his straw hat.

"Superintendent Maigret?"

"Yes."

"I'm Inspector Benoit. . . . It was my colleague, whom I've just relieved, who got your message at noon. The superintendent of the airport apologizes for not being here to welcome you. He's been called to Nice on urgent business."

Some distance ahead of them, passengers were hurrying toward the buildings; the concrete runway was hot, and in the sunshine they could see a crowd of people behind a barrier, waving handkerchiefs.

"We were a little worried about what to do just now, and after asking the super's advice I took the liberty of calling the Quai des Orfèvres. I got an officer called Lucas on the phone and he told me he knew about the case. The woman in whom you're interested . . ."

He glanced at a piece of paper he had in his hand.

". . . Countess Paverini arrived just in time to catch the Swissair plane. Since I didn't have any orders I didn't want to detain her on my own authority. The superintendent didn't know what to do either. That's why I called police headquarters first and Inspector Lucas . . ."

"Sergeant . . ."

"Sergeant Lucas, sorry, seemed as worried as me. The lady wasn't alone. She had an important-looking gentleman with her who'd brought her in his car and had called half an hour earlier to reserve a seat for her on the plane to Geneva."

"Van Meulen?"

"I don't know. They can tell you at the office."

"In short, you let her get away?"

"Was I wrong?"

Maigret did not reply immediately.

"No, I don't think so . . . ," he sighed at last. "When's there another plane for Geneva?"

"There's none before tomorrow morning. But, if you've absolutely got to get there, there's another way. Just the day before yesterday we had somebody in the same fix. If you take the two-forty plane for Rome you'll be in time for the Rome-Geneva-Paris-London plane and . . ."

Maigret nearly burst out laughing, for he suddenly had the impression that he was behind the times. To travel from Nice to Geneva you merely had to go to Rome and from there . . .

In the bar, just as at Orly, he saw pilots and stewardesses, Americans, Italians, Spaniards. A child of four who had traveled alone from New York and who was being handed from one hostess to another was solemnly eating ice cream.

"I'd like to make a telephone call."

The inspector did him the honors of the tiny police office, where everyone knew by now who he was and looked at him with curiosity.

"What's the number, Superintendent?"

"The Hotel de Paris at Monte Carlo."

A few minutes later he knew, through the concierge at the Hotel de Paris, that Monsieur Joseph Van Meulen was indeed staying at the hotel, that he had been summoned to Nice by a telephone call, had gone there with his car and his chauffeur, had been away for a short time, and had only just returned.

He was now having a bath, and he had reserved a table for the gala dinner that evening at the Sporting Club.

Nobody had seen the Countess Paverini, who was well known at the hotel. As for Mademoiselle Nadine, she had not accompanied Van Meulen when he left in his car.

Who was Nadine? Maigret had no idea. The concierge, however, seemed to assume that the entire world knew about her, and Maigret avoided asking any questions.

"Will you take the plane to Rome?" asked the young policeman from Nice.

"No. I'll reserve a seat on the Swissair plane for tomorrow morning and I'll probably spend the night at Monte Carlo."

"I'll take you over to Swissair."

It was a desk beside other desks in the hall.

"Do you know Countess Paverini?"

"She's a good customer of ours. She took the plane for Geneva a short while ago."

"Do you know where she stays in Geneva?"

"Usually she doesn't stop in Geneva, but at Lausanne. We've frequently sent her tickets to the Lausanne-Palace."

Maigret suddenly felt that Paris was very large, but that the world was very small. It took him almost as long to go by car to Monte Carlo as it had taken him to come from Orly.

*In which
Maigret meets
another multimillionaire,
as naked as the first,
but alive and well*

Here, too, they seemed anxious to keep quiet about the presence of the police. On entering the lobby, Maigret recognized the concierge, whom he had phoned from the airport, and with whom, as he realized on seeing him, he had been in contact more than once when the man was employed in a grand hotel on the Champs-Élysées. At that time he had not sitting in state at the reception desk wearing a frock coat, but had been an ordinary bellboy waiting to hurry forward at his guests' beck and call.

In the lobby there were still some people in beach wear, while others were in evening dress, and in front of Maigret a large half-naked woman with a scarlet back, carrying a small dog under her arm, exuded a powerful smell of suntan oil.

The concierge was careful not to address Maigret by his name and, above all, not to call him superintendent, but instead gave him a knowing wink as he said:

"Just a second . . . I've been working on it. . . ."

Then he unhooked the receiver: "Hello . . . Monsieur Jean? . . ."

Telephones in this hotel must have been particularly sensitive, for the concierge spoke in almost a whisper: "The person I mentioned has come. . . . Shall I send him up? . . . All right . . ."

And to Maigret: "Monsieur Van Meulen's secretary will be waiting for you at the gate of the elevator, fifth floor, and he'll take you up. . . ."

It was as though Maigret was having a favor bestowed upon him. A dapper young man was, as arranged, waiting for him in the corridor.

"Monsieur Joseph Van Meulen offers his apologies for receiving you while he has his massage, because he has to go out immediately afterward. He asks me to tell you that he is delighted to meet you in the flesh, for he has followed some of your investigations with the greatest interest."

Wasn't this a little odd? Why couldn't the Belgian financier tell him that himself, since they were going to meet in a moment?

Maigret was taken into a suite that so closely resembled those in the George V—the same furniture, arranged in the same way—that he would have imagined he was still in Paris if he hadn't seen the harbor and the yachts through the window.

"Superintendent Maigret," announced Monsieur Jean, opening the bedroom door.

"Come in, Superintendent, sit down and make yourself comfortable," said a man lying on his stomach, completely naked, who was being kneaded by a masseur in white trousers and a T shirt revealing enormous biceps. "I expected a visit like this, but I thought I would get merely a local inspector. That you should have taken the trouble to come personally . . ."

He did not complete his remark. This was the second multimillionaire Maigret had met in one day, and he was stark naked, like the first, which in no way seemed to embarrass him.

On the photographs he had found in the cookie tin, many people were scantily clad, as though above a certain social level different standards of decency prevailed.

This man appeared to be very tall, with hardly any excess flesh, sun-tanned all over except for a narrow band of skin that had been protected by his trunks and that looked uncomfortably white. The superintendent could not see his face, which was buried in a pillow, but his tanned skull was bald and smooth.

Ignoring the presence of the masseur, who presumably didn't count for him, the Belgian went on:

"I knew, of course, that you would pick up Louise's trail and I warned her myself this morning on the telephone not to try and hide. Note that I know nothing about what happened. She didn't dare tell me any details over the phone. Besides, she was in such a state . . . Do you know her?"

"No."

"She's a funny creature, one of the oddest and most engaging women in the world. . . . Finished, Bob?"

"Just two more minutes, monsieur."

The masseur must have been an ex-boxer, for he had a broken nose and cauliflower ears. There were beads of sweat on the black hairs on his forearms and the backs of his hands.

"I suppose you're in touch with Paris? What's the latest news?"

"The investigation has really just begun," Maigret replied cautiously.

"I don't mean the investigation. What about the papers? Have they published the news?"

"Not as far as I know."

"I'll be surprised if one of the Philps brothers at least, probably the younger, hasn't already taken the plane for Paris."

"Who could have given them the information?"

"Arnold, of course. And as soon as the women get to know . . ."

"You're referring to the Colonel's former wives?"

"They're the most interested parties, surely? I don't know where Dorothy is, but Alice must be in Paris, and Muriel, who lives in Lausanne, will jump on the first plane. . . . That's enough, Bob. . . . Thanks . . . tomorrow at the same time . . . no! I've got an engagement. Say four o'clock?"

The masseur had laid a yellow towel over the man's back and Van Meulen got up slowly, wrapping it around him like an apron. He stood up; he was indeed a very tall man, powerfully built and muscular, in perfect physical condition for a man of sixty-five or seventy. He stared at the superintendent with unconcealed curiosity.

"I'm glad. . . ." he said without explaining himself further. "You don't mind if I get dressed in front of you? I've got to, because I'm giving twenty people dinner at tonight's gala. I'll have a quick shower."

He went into the bathroom and there was the sound of running water. The masseur packed his things in a case, put on a colored jacket, and left; he, too, had glanced at Maigret with curiosity.

Van Meulen was soon back, clad in a bathrobe, water still gleaming on his face and on his bald head. His dinner jacket, white silk shirt, socks and shoes—all the things he was going to wear were laid out on an ingenious coat hanger of a type unfamiliar to Maigret.

"David was a good friend of mine, an old partner, I might say, because we'd known each other for over thirty years—thirty-eight, to be precise—and we'd shared an interest in a number of concerns. . . . The news of his death came as a real shock, especially a death of that kind."

What was surprising was the absolute naturalness of his behavior; Maigret couldn't remember ever seeing anything like it. He went back and forth, getting ready exactly as if he had been all alone and were talking to himself.

This was the man whom the little Countess called "Daddy," and the superintendent had begun to see why. He was so obviously strong and reliable. The young secretary had gone into the next room to make a phone call. A waiter whom nobody had rung for brought in a misted glass of some transparent liquid, presumably a Martini, on a silver tray. Drinks at this hour must form part of a regular cycle of habits.

"Thanks, Ludo. Can I offer you something, Maigret?"

He said neither "superintendent" nor "monsieur," and yet there was nothing offensive about it. It seemed, rather, a way of putting them on equal footing.

"I'll have the same as you."

"Very dry?"

Maigret nodded. His interlocutor had already slipped on

his underpants, his waistcoat, and his black silk socks, and was looking around for the shoehorn before putting on his patent-leather shoes.

"Have you ever met her?"

"Countess Paverini, you mean?"

"Yes, Louise . . . If you don't know her yet you'll find it hard to understand. . . . You've had a lot of experience with men, I know, but I wonder if you're equally good at understanding women. . . . Are you planning to go and see her at Lausanne?"

There was no hanky-panky, no attempt to pretend that the Countess was anywhere else.

"She'll have had time to calm down a little. . . . This morning when she called me from the hospital she was talking so incoherently that I told her to get into the first plane and come over to see me."

"You were married to her, weren't you?"

"For two and a half years. We're still good friends. Why shouldn't we be? It's a miracle that the hotel nurse thought of putting some of Louise's clothes and her handbag into the ambulance; otherwise she wouldn't have been able to leave the nursing home. There was no money in the purse, only a little small change. At Orly she had to pay her taxi by check, and that wasn't too easy. . . . In short, I had her met at the airport and we had a bite to eat in Nice, where she told me her story."

Maigret avoided asking any questions, choosing rather to let the other man talk as he pleased.

"I assume you don't suspect her of killing David?"

When Maigret didn't answer, Van Meulen looked grave.

"That would be a big mistake, Maigret, I tell you that as a

friend. And to begin with, let me ask you a question. Is it certain that somebody held David's head under water in the tub?"

"Who told you about that?"

"Louise, of course."

"She saw him?"

"She saw him, and she doesn't attempt to deny it. . . . Were you unaware of that? . . . Jean, would you give me my studs and cuff links?"

He suddenly seemed a worried man.

"Listen, Maigret, I'd better set you straight before you go off on a wild-goose chase, and I'd like to spare Louise any unnecessary trouble. She's still a little girl. Even though she's thirty-nine she is, and always will be, a child. That's what gives her her charm, in fact. And that's what continually gets her into impossible situations."

The secretary helped him insert his platinum cuff links, and Van Meulen sat down opposite the superintendent as though allowing himself a moment's respite.

"Louise's father was a general, and her mother's family were provincial gentry. I believe she was born in Morocco, where her father was posted, but she spent a large part of her youth in Nancy. She was already longing to be independent and she persuaded her parents to let her go to Paris to study art history. . . . To your health."

Maigret drank a mouthful of Martini and looked around for a table on which to set his glass.

"Put it on the floor, anywhere. . . . She met an Italian, Count Marco Paverini, and fell head over heels in love. Do you know Paverini?"

"No."

"You will."

He seemed quite sure of it.

"He's a real Count, but penniless. As far as I know he was living at that time on the favors of an older woman. Louise's parents, at Nancy, took a lot of persuading; Louise gilded the pill so effectively that they ended up giving their consent to the marriage. Let's call that the first stage, when people had begun to call her "the little Countess." They had an apartment in Passy, then a room in a hotel, then another apartment, various ups and downs, but they never failed to appear at cocktail parties, receptions, and entertainments."

"Did Paverini make use of his wife?"

Van Meulen had the honesty to hesitate.

"No. Not in the way you think. She wouldn't have gone along with it anyway. She was madly in love and still is. It's getting harder to understand, isn't it? And yet it's the truth. I'm even convinced that Marco is in love with her too, that in any case he can't do without her.

"Nevertheless they were always quarreling. She left him three or four times after violent scenes, but never for more than a few days. Marco only had to reappear looking pale and distraught, and beg her forgiveness, for her to fall into his arms again."

"What did they live on?"

Van Meulen gave an imperceptible shrug of the shoulders.

"*You're* asking me that? What do so many of one's acquaintances live on? It was after one of those fights that I met her. I felt very sorry for her. I thought it was the wrong kind of life for her, that she was wearing herself out, that she'd soon lose all her charm in the hands of a man like

74

Marco, and since I'd recently been divorced I asked her to marry me."

"Were you in love?"

Van Meulen looked at him in silence and his eyes seemed to be repeating the question.

"The same thing has happened several times in my life, as it happened to David. Does that answer your question? I won't conceal the fact that I had a talk with Marco and gave him a large check to make himself scarce in South America."

"Did he accept?"

"I had certain means of persuading him."

"I suppose he had done something . . . unscrupulous?"

Another barely perceptible shrug.

"Louise was my wife for almost three years and I was fairly happy with her. . . ."

"Did you know she still loved Marco?"

Van Meulen's expression implied, So what? He went on: "She went around with me everywhere. I travel a great deal. She met my friends, some of whom she already knew. There were occasional clouds, of course, and even some bad storms. . . . I believe she was, and still is, really fond of me. . . . She calls me Daddy, which doesn't bother me, since after all I'm thirty years older than she is."

"Was it through you that she met David Ward?"

"It was through me, as you say."

There was a flicker of irony in his eyes.

"It wasn't David who took her away from me, but Marco, who came back one day looking thin and miserable, and began to hang around on the sidewalk opposite looking like a stray dog. . . . One evening she fell on my neck in a fit of weeping and confessed. . . ."

The telephone had rung in the next room and the secretary, who had answered the call, appeared in the doorway.

"Mr. Philps is on the line."

"Donald or Herbert?"

"Donald . . ."

"What did I tell you? The younger Philps. Is he calling from Paris?"

"Yes."

"I'll take it. . . ."

He reached out for the receiver, and the conversation took place in English. Van Meulen replied to the questions he was being asked over the phone with:

"Yes . . . No . . . I don't know yet. . . . Apparently there's no doubt about it. . . . Superintendent Maigret, who's in charge, is right here with me. . . . Certainly I'll go to Paris for the funeral, although it couldn't be more inconvenient, since I was to have left for Ceylon the day after tomorrow. . . . Hello! . . . Are you at the George V? . . . If I find out anything I'll call you back. . . . No, tonight I'll be out and I won't be back before three in the morning. . . . Good-by."

He looked at Maigret.

"Well, it happened. Philps is there, as I'd predicted. He's in a highly excited state. The English papers have heard the news and he's being besieged by reporters. . . . What was I saying? I really must finish dressing . . . my ties, Jean . . ."

The secretary brought him half a dozen to choose from; they all looked identical, but he examined them carefully before selecting one.

"What could I have done? I offered to divorce her, and so that Marco wouldn't leave her penniless one day, I gave her a modest allowance instead of a lump sum."

"You continued to see her?"

"Seeing both of them. . . . Does that surprise you?"

He was fastening his bow tie at the mirror, his neck stretched out and his Adam's apple protruding.

"As was to be expected, the scenes began again. Then one fine day David got divorced from Muriel, and it was his turn to play the good Samaritan."

"He didn't marry her, though?"

"He didn't have time to. He was waiting for the divorce proceedings to be completed. . . . I wonder, come to think of it, what's going to happen. . . . I don't know exactly how far they got but if all the papers have not been signed, it's probable that Muriel Halligan would be considered David's widow."

"Is that all you know?"

He replied, simply:

"No. I also know, in part anyway, what happened last night, and you may as well hear it from me as from Louise. Above all, I want to impress on you that she did not kill David Ward. To begin with, she would probably have been incapable of it. . . ."

"Physically?"

"That's what I mean by the word, yes. Morally, if I may use that term, we are all capable of killing, provided we have an adequate motive and can feel sure of not being caught."

"An adequate motive?"

"Passion, for a start. One has to believe that, since we're constantly seeing men and women committing crimes of passion. . . . Although my opinion on that subject . . . But that's neither here nor there. . . . Self-interest . . . If it's sufficiently in someone's interest . . . But this was not the case with Louise, quite the reverse."

"Unless Ward had made a will in her favor or . . ."

"There's no will in her favor, believe me. . . . David is an Englishman, and consequently he keeps his head and assesses everything at its proper value."

"Was he in love with the Countess?"

Van Meulen frowned irritably.

"That's the third or fourth time you've used that word, Maigret. Try to understand. David was my age. Louise is a pretty little creature, amusing, even fascinating. Moreover, she has done her homework, if I may express myself so. That is to say, she had picked up the habits of a certain social set, a certain way of life. . . ."

"I think I understand."

"Then I don't need to elaborate. I don't claim that it's very high-minded, but it's human. Journalists don't understand, they just build a romance out of any of our affairs. . . . Jean, my checkbook . . ."

He had only his dinner jacket to put on, and he was looking at his watch.

"Last night they dined in town, then went together for a drink at some night club, I didn't ask her which. It so happened that they met Marco with a big blonde Dutchwoman who belongs to the top social set. They just greeted one another from a distance. Marco danced with his partner. Louise was on edge, and when she got back to the George V with David she told him in the elevator that she wanted another bottle of champagne.

"Does she drink a lot?"

"Too much. David drank too much too, but only at night. They sat talking, each of them with a bottle, for David drank only Scotch, and I would guess that by the end of their conversation had begun to be incoherent. After a few drinks Louise tends to develop a guilt complex and to accuse herself of all imaginable sins. . . . According to what she told me today, she declared to David that she was unworthy of him, that she despised herself for being a poor, crazy female, but that she couldn't help running after Marco and begging him to take her back."

"What did Ward say?"

"Nothing. It's even doubtful whether he understood. That's why I asked you whether there was any proof that somebody had held him down in the bathtub. Until midnight or one o'clock he would have been all right, because he only started drinking at five in the afternoon. By about two in the morning he would become fuddled, and I often thought he might have an accident when he took a bath. I even advised him to have a manservant within reach at all times, but he hated feeling dependent on people. For the same reason, he insisted that Arnold live in a different hotel. I wonder if it wasn't out of a kind of shyness.

"Well, that's about all. Louise got undressed and put on her dressing gown, and it's possible that since the champagne bottle was empty she might have had a shot of whisky. Then she started thinking that she must have upset David, and she wanted to go and beg his forgiveness. That's really in character, believe me, I know her well. . . . She went down the hall. She swore to me that she found the door ajar. She went in. In the bathroom she saw what you did, and instead of calling for help she ran back to her room and flung herself down on her bed. She claims that at that point she really wanted to die, and it's certainly possible. . . .

"So she took some of her sleeping pills, which she was already taking in my day, especially when she had been drinking."

"How many pills?"

"I can guess what you're thinking. You may be right. She wanted to die, because that would settle everything, but she wouldn't have minded going on living. The intention was enough; it produced the same effect. The fact remains that she rang the bell in time. . . . Put yourself in her place. . . . It was all a kind of nightmare to her in which reality and unreality were hopelessly confused.

"At the nursing home, when she regained consciousness, it was harsh reality that prevailed. Her first thought was to call Marco, and she dialed his number. Nobody answered. Then she called a hotel on Rue de Ponthieu where he sometimes stays when he's in funds. He wasn't there either. . . . She thought of me. She told me incoherently that she was done for, that David was dead, that she had almost died herself, and that she wished she had, and she begged me to come immediately.

"I told her it was impossible. After trying in vain to get more details out of her I advised her to go to Orly and take the plane for Nice.

"That's all, Maigret. I sent her to Lausanne, where she feels at home, not to hide her from the police, but to save her from being hounded by journalists and busybodies, and from all the complications that are bound to ensue.

"You tell me that David was murdered and I believe you.

"And I say that it wasn't Louise who killed him and that I don't have the slightest idea who did. . . . And now . . ."

He finally put on his dinner jacket.

"If there are any calls for me, I'm at the Sporting Club," he told his secretary.

"What should I do if it's from New York?"

"Tell them I've thought it over and my answer is no."

"All right, monsieur."

"Coming, Maigret?"

They took the elevator together, and when they reached the ground floor they were unpleasantly surprised by the blinding flash of a camera.

"I should have known. . . ," growled Van Meulen.

And pushing aside a fat little man who was standing beside the photographer trying to bar his way, he hurried to the exit.

"Superintendent Maigret?"

The little man was a reporter from a local paper.

"Couldn't we have a little chat?"

The concierge was watching them from a distance with a frown.

"We could sit down in a corner. . . ."

Maigret had enough experience to know that it was no use trying to escape; then statements would be imputed to him that he had never made.

"I suppose I can't offer you a drink at the bar?" continued the journalist.

"I've just had one."

"With Joseph Van Meulen?"

"Yes."

"Is it true that Countess Paverini was down here this afternoon?"

"That's right."

The superintendent had sat down in a huge leather armchair, and the reporter, notebook in hand, sat in front of him, perched on the edge of a chair.

"I suppose she's the number one suspect?"

"Why?"

"That's what they told us on the phone from Paris."

Somebody must have alerted the press, from the George V or from the airport—possibly one of the Orly inspectors in collusion with a newspaper?

"You just missed her?"

"That's to say, when I reached Nice she had already left."

"For Lausanne, I know."

The press had wasted no time.

"I've just been on the phone to the Lausanne-Palace. She arrived there from Geneva in a taxi. She seemed exhausted. She refused to answer any questions from the reporters who were waiting for her, and went right up to her suite, number 214."

The journalist seemed pleased at being able to give Maigret these details.

"She had a bottle of champagne brought up, then she sent for a doctor, who's due there any minute. Do you believe she killed the Colonel?"

"I'm not as quick a worker as you and your friends."

"Are you going to Lausanne?"

"Maybe."

"On the morning plane tomorrow? You know that the

82

Colonel's third wife lives in Lausanne and that she and
Countess Paverini can't stand one another?"

"I didn't know that."

It was a strange interview, in which the reporter was providing the news.

"Suppose she's guilty, I guess you won't have the right to
arrest her?"

"Not without an extradition order."

"I guess that to get it you'd have to submit formal evidence?"

"Look, I have the impression you're making up your story
and I don't advise you to write it in this vein. There's no
question of arresting or extraditing anybody. . . ."

"The Countess isn't a suspect?"

"I have no idea."

"So, then . . ."

This time Maigret lost his temper.

"No!" he almost shouted, making the concierge jump. "I
have told you nothing, for the good reason that I know nothing, and if you put any ambiguous remarks into my mouth
like the ones you've been making you'll be sorry. . . ."

"But . . ."

"Not a word!" he said abruptly, getting up and heading
for the bar.

He was so furious that he ordered a Martini almost without being aware of it.

The bartender must have recognized Maigret from his
photographs, because he looked at him with some curiosity.
Two or three customers perched on their stools turned
around to stare at him. In spite of the concierge's precautions, everyone already knew that he was at the hotel.

"Where are the phone booths?"

"On the left, in the corridor. . . ."

Feeling very irritable, he shut himself up in the first one he came to.

"Get me Paris, please. . . . Danton four four two oh . . ."

The lines weren't busy and Maigret only had to wait five minutes. He paced up and down the hall. He was called back before the five minutes were up.

"Department of Criminal Investigation? . . . Get me the inspectors' office. This is Maigret. . . . Hello! Is Lucas still there?"

He guessed that Lucas, good man, would have had a busy day, too, and would not be going home early.

"Is that you, Chief?"

"Yes, I'm in Monte Carlo. . . . Any news?"

"You know, of course, that in spite of all our precautions the press has gotten wind of things?"

"I know, yes."

"The third edition of *France-Soir* came out with a big front-page article. At four o'clock this afternoon English journalists came over from London at the same time as a Mr. Philps, some kind of lawyer . . ."

"A solicitor . . ."

"That's it. . . . He insisted on a personal interview with the Big Chief. . . . They were closeted together for over an hour. When he came out he was surrounded, interviewed, and photographed, and he hit one photographer with his umbrella trying to smash his camera."

"Is that all?"

"They're saying that Countess Paverini, Ward's mistress, may have committed the crime, and that you're personally

84

on her trail. I was called by a certain John Arnold. He's hopping mad."

"Next?"

"The journalists invaded the George V, and the hotel detectives had to throw them out."

"Where's Lapointe?"

"He's here. He wants to talk to you . . . I'll put him on."

Lapointe's voice: "Hello, Chief. . . . I went to the American Hospital at Neuilly as planned. . . . I questioned the nurse and the switchboard girl. Then I found out from the receptionist that when she left Countess Paverini had given her a letter to mail. It was addressed to Count Marco Paverini, on Rue de l'Etoile. . . . Since I had found out nothing of interest at the hospital I went to that address. It's quite an elegant apartment house. I talked to the landlady, who began by raising various objections. Apparently Count Paverini did not sleep at home last night, which is not unusual for him. He came back about eleven this morning, looking worried, without even checking at the concierge's lodge to see if there was any mail for him. Less than half an hour later he went out again, carrying a small suitcase. He hasn't been heard from since."

Maigret said nothing, because he had nothing to say, and Lapointe, at the other end of the line, was obviously baffled.

"What should I do? Should I keep looking for him?"

"If you feel like it . . ."

The answer was calculated to bewilder Lapointe still further.

"Don't you think . . . ?"

What had Van Meulen said to him a little while ago? Anyone is capable of committing murder provided they have an adequate motive. Passion . . . Could that be the case here, when Louise had been someone else's wife for three years and the Colonel's mistress for over a year? Wasn't she in fact on the point of leaving the latter to go back to her first husband?

Interest? What did Paverini have to gain from Ward's death?

Maigret was somewhat discouraged, as he often was at the start of an investigation. There is always a moment when the protagonists appear unreal and their actions incoherent.

During such periods Maigret tended to become sullen, stolid, almost dull. Young Lapointe, although the newest member of the team, was beginning to know him well enough to realize, even over the telephone, what was happening.

"I'll do my best, Chief. I've made a list of the people who are on the photographs. There are only two or three still to be identified."

The air was stifling in the phone booth, especially since Maigret was not dressed for the Riviera. He went to finish his drink at the bar, and noticed tables set for dinner on the terrace.

"Can I get some dinner?"

"Yes, but I'm afraid those tables are all reserved. They are every evening. You can have a table inside."

Of course! If they had dared, they would probably have sent him to eat with the staff!

*In which
Maigret at last
meets somebody
who has no money
and who is worried*

He slept badly, never completely losing consciousness of his surroundings, of the hotel with its two hundred open windows, the public garden with its lawns blue-gray in the lamplight, the casino that was as old-fashioned as the elderly ladies in out-of-date dresses he had seen entering it after dinner, and the lazy sea that, every twelve seconds—he had counted them over and over again, as other people count sheep—broke into a rippling fringe of foam on the rocky shore.

Cars stopped and started up again, performing complicated maneuvers. Car doors slammed. Voices sounded so distinct that he felt like an eavesdropper, and there were still some noisy buses bringing batches of gamblers and taking others away, while the music went on playing on the terrace of the Café de Paris across the street.

When by some miracle a brief silence fell, he could hear in the background, like the sound of a flute in an orchestra, the faint, anachronistic noise of a carriage.

He had left his window open because of the heat. But since he had brought no luggage and had gone to bed without pajamas, he soon felt chilled and went to close it, casting a resentful glance at the distant lights of the Sporting Club, where Joseph Van Meulen, the little Countess's "Daddy," was presiding over a table set for twenty.

Because of his change of mood, he now saw people in a different light, and he felt annoyed with himself, almost humiliated at having listened so meekly to the Belgian financier, as though not daring to interrupt him.

Hadn't he basically been flattered that such a well-bred person had treated him with friendly familiarity? Unlike John Arnold, the plump little Englishman with his irritating self-confidence, Van Meulen had not appeared to be giving him a lecture on the habits of a certain social set, and had indeed seemed impressed at receiving a personal visit from Maigret.

"I know *you* can understand me," he had seemed to be saying all the time. Had Maigret allowed himself to be taken in? *Daddy . . . the little Countess . . . David . . .* and all the other Christian names these people used without bothering about further details, as though it was up to everybody else to recognize them.

He dozed off a little, rolled over clumsily, and suddenly saw, in his mind's eye, the colonel lying naked in his tub, then the Belgian, equally naked, being pummeled by a masseur who looked like a boxer.

Weren't these men too highly civilized to fall under suspicion?

"We are all capable of killing, provided we have an adequate motive and can feel sure of not being caught. . . ."

Van Meulen, however, had not considered passion an adequate motive. Hadn't he subtly implied that in some cases passion is almost inconceivable?

"At our age . . . a young, attractive woman who has done her homework . . ."

Their little Countess sent for the doctor, groaned, let herself be taken to hospital, then, on the sly, telephoned first to try and get hold of her first husband, who was still intermittently her lover, and then her kind "Daddy," Van Meulen.

She knew Ward was dead. She had seen the corpse. The poor little thing didn't know which way to turn.

Should she call the police? That was out of the question. Her nerves were too shaken. And how could policemen, with their heavy boots and narrow minds, understand the sort of thing that went on in her set?

"Take the plane, my dear. Come and see me and I'll advise you. . . ."

And meanwhile that other character, John Arnold, was at the Hotel George V lavishing advice and barely disguised threats.

"Be extremely careful. Don't let the press know. Watch your step. This case is dynamite. There are big interests at stake. There'll be worldwide repercussions."

At the same time, he had been calling lawyers in London, urging them to come over, presumably to help him cover things up.

Van Meulen had deliberately sent Countess Paverini off to Lausanne to rest, as though this were the natural and proper thing to do. She hadn't been running away, of course. She was not trying to evade the police.

"I sent her to Lausanne, where she feels at home. . . . To

91

save her from being hounded by journalists . . . and all the complications that are bound to ensue. . . ."

And so it was Maigret who had to bestir himself and take the plane once more. . . .

Maigret hated prejudice. His judgment of people did not depend on whether they had too much money or too little. He was anxious to remain cool, but he could not help being irritated by innumerable details.

He heard the guests returning from the famous gala dinner, talking in loud voices outside and then inside the hotel, the sound of running water and flushing toilets.

He was up before anyone else the next morning, by six o'clock, and he shaved with the cheap razor he had asked a bellboy to buy for him, together with a toothbrush. It took him almost half an hour to get a cup of coffee. As he went through the hall, he saw cleaners at work. When he asked for his bill the weary reception clerk told him: "Monsieur Van Meulen said . . ."

"Never mind what Monsieur Van Meulen said."

He insisted on paying. Outside the door the Belgian financier's Rolls was waiting, the chauffeur holding open the door.

"Monsieur Van Meulen has told me to take you to the airport. . . ."

He did get into the car all the same because he had never ridden in a Rolls. He arrived early at the airport and bought some newspapers. On the front page of the local paper there was a picture of himself and Van Meulen leaving the elevator, with the caption: "Superintendent Maigret after a conference with the multimillionaire Van Meulen."

A conference!

The Paris papers headlined in heavy type:

ENGLISH MULTIMILLIONAIRE FOUND DEAD IN BATH

They were certainly splashing the millionaire side of it!

### CRIME OR ACCIDENT?

Presumably the journalists were not yet up, for he was allowed to take off in peace. He fastened his seat belt, stared vaguely through the window at the sea as it grew distant, and at the little white red-roofed houses scattered over the dark-green of the mountainside.

"Coffee or tea?"

He seemed to be sulking; the stewardess fussing over him didn't even earn a smile, and when, under a cloudless sky, he beheld the Alps beneath him, he refused to admit that the sight was a magnificent one.

Actually, less than ten minutes later, they ran into a fine mist that streamed alongside the plane and soon turned into dense vapor, like the hissing steam that pours out of railway engines.

In Geneva it was raining. It wasn't just starting to rain, it had been raining for a long time—one could feel that—it was cold and people were wearing raincoats.

Scarcely had he set foot on the gangway when flashes broke out. Though the journalists had not been there to see him off, they were waiting for him to arrive, seven or eight of them with notebooks and questions.

"I have nothing to say. . . ."

"Are you going to Lausanne?"

"I don't know. . . ."

He brushed them aside with the kind help of a representative of Swissair who piloted him through the back passages of the air terminal to spare him formalities and standing in line.

"Do you have a car? Are you taking the train to Lausanne?"

"I think I'll take a taxi."

"I'll call one."

Two cars followed his, crammed with reporters and photographers. Still feeling irritable, he tried to doze in a corner, casting a vague glance from time to time over the wet vineyards and the stretches of gray lake water to be glimpsed between the trees.

What annoyed him most was the sense that his movements had been more or less decided for him. He was not going to Lausanne because he had decided so himself, but because a path had been mapped out for him that led there whether he liked it or not.

His taxi pulled up in front of the colonnade of the Lausanne-Palace. Photographers bombarded him. He was questioned. The doorman helped him thread his way through.

Inside, he found the same atmosphere as in the George V or the Hotel de Paris. Apparently people who do a lot of traveling like to keep to the same setting. The décor here was possibly a little heavier and more sober, with a concierge in a black frock coat discreetly trimmed with gold who spoke five or six languages like all the others, the only difference being that his French betrayed a slight German accent.

"Is Countess Paverini here?"

"Yes, *Monsieur le Commissaire*. In number 214, as usual."

In the lounge an Asiatic family sat waiting for Heaven

knows what, a woman in a gilded sari, and three children with huge dark eyes staring at him with curiosity.

It was barely ten o'clock in the morning.

"I suppose she's not up yet?"

"She rang for her breakfast half an hour ago. Shall I let her know you're here? I think she's expecting you."

"Do you know if she has made or received any telephone calls?"

"You'd better ask at the switchboard. . . . Hans, take the superintendent to the switchboard."

It was at the end of a hall behind the reception desk. Three women, side by side, were fiddling with telephone plugs.

"Can you tell me . . ."

"One moment, please . . ."

And in English: "Your call to Bangkok, monsieur . . ."

"Can you tell me whether Countess Paverini has made or received any calls since she's been here?"

They had lists in front of them.

"At one o'clock this morning she had a call from Monte Carlo."

Van Meulen, of course, "Daddy," who between a couple of dances at the Sporting Club, or more likely between two runs of luck at the gaming table, had taken the trouble to phone to see how she was.

"This morning she called Paris. . . ."

"What number?"

It was the number of Marco's bachelor apartment on Rue de l'Etoile.

"Did she get an answer?"

"No. She left a message asking to be called back."

"Anything else?"

"About ten minutes ago she asked for Monte Carlo again."

"Did she get through?"

"Yes. Six minutes."

"Will you let her know I'm here?"

"Of course, Monsieur Maigret."

It was idiotic. He had heard so much about her that he felt a certain sense of excitement, and this humiliated him. Going up in the elevator, he felt like a young man about to meet a famous actress in person for the first time.

"This way . . ."

The bellboy knocked at a door. A voice said, "Come in." When the door was opened Maigret found himself in a living room whose two windows overlooked the lake.

There was no one there. A voice spoke from the adjoining room, the door of which was ajar.

"Sit down, *Monsieur le Commissaire*. I'll be with you in a minute."

On a tray were eggs and bacon that had hardly been touched, rolls and a crumbled *croissant*. He thought he caught the characteristic sound of a bottle being recorked. At last there came a rustle of silk.

"Forgive me. . . ."

And, as happens to the young man who disturbs an actress in her dressing room, he felt a sense of confusion and disappointment. There stood before him a very ordinary little person, her face scarcely made up, pale skinned and heavy eyed, holding out a damp, shaky hand to him.

"Please do sit down"

Through the half-open door he had time to glimpse an

unmade bed, things untidily strewn around, a bottle of medicine on the bedside table.

She sat down opposite him, folding the edges of a cream-colored silk dressing gown over her legs; her nightgown showed through the thin material.

"I'm sorry to have given you all this trouble."

She looked every day of her thirty-nine years, and at this moment even a little more. Her eyes were ringed with dark bluish shadows and there was a tiny crease running down beside each nostril.

She was not feigning weariness. She really was exhausted, at the end of her rope, about to burst into tears, he could have sworn. She was looking at him not knowing what to say when the telephone rang.

"May I?"

"Please do."

"Hello! Yes, speaking . . . You can put her through to me. . . . Yes, Anne . . . How kind of you to call me. . . . Thank you. . . . Yes . . . I don't know yet. . . . I have somebody with me at the moment. . . . No. Don't ask me to go out. . . . Yes . . . Tell Her Highness. . . . Thank you. . . . Good-by. . . ."

Tiny drops of sweat were beading on her upper lips, and as she spoke Maigret caught a whiff of alcohol.

"Are you very angry with me?"

She was not being affected, however, she seemed quite natural, much too shaken to have the courage to play a role.

"It's so horrible, so unexpected! And on the very day when . . ."

"When you were going to tell Colonel Ward that you had decided to leave him? Isn't that what you were going to say?"

She nodded.

"I think Jef . . . I think Van Meulen told you all about it, didn't he? I wonder what more I can tell you. Are you going to take me back to Paris?"

"Does that frighten you?"

"I don't know. . . . He advised me to go with you if that was what you wanted. I do whatever he tells me . . . He's such a wonderful man, so kind and so intelligent! You feel he knows everything, foresees everything. . . ."

"He didn't foresee the death of his friend Ward."

"But he did foresee that I'd go back to Marco."

"Was anything settled between Marco and yourself? I thought that when you came face to face with your first husband in the night club he was with a young Dutchwoman and that you didn't speak to him. . . ."

"That's true. But I had made up my mind anyway."

Her hands, which looked older than her face, were twitching nervously, and she was wringing her fingers, leaving white marks over the knuckles.

"How can you expect me to explain it when I don't know myself? Things were going so well, I thought I was cured; David and I were going to get married as soon as the final divorce documents were signed. . . . David was the same sort of man as Van Meulen, not quite the same but somewhat like . . ."

"What do you mean by that?"

"With Daddy, I have the feeling that he always tells me what he's thinking. . . . Not necessarily everything, since he doesn't want to bother me with details. . . . I feel in direct contact, you understand? David, on the other hand, used to watch me with a twinkle in those big round eyes of his.

98

Perhaps he wasn't making fun of me but of himself. . . . He was like a big, wise, cunning cat . . ."

Again she said: "You understand?"

"Earlier that evening, when you went out to dinner with the Colonel, you had no intention of leaving him?"

She thought for a moment.

"No."

Then she corrected herself: "But I suspected it would happen some day."

"Why?"

"Because it had happened before. I didn't want to go back to Marco, because I knew . . ."

She bit her lip.

"What did you know?"

"That it would begin all over again. He has no money, neither do I. . . ."

She suddenly launched out on a new idea, speaking in the quick, jerky manner of someone under the influence of a drug.

"I'm not rich, did you know? I have nothing at all. If Van Meulen hadn't sent money to the bank this morning, the check I wrote at the airport would have bounced. He had to give me some yesterday so I could come here. I'm very poor. . . ."

"Your jewelry . . ."

"Some jewelry, yes . . . And my mink . . . That's all!"

She sighed, as though despairing of making herself understood.

"It wasn't as you imagine. . . . He paid for my lodging, my bills, my travels. But I never had any money in my bag. As long as I was with him I didn't need it. . . ."

"Whereas if you'd been married . . ."

"It would have been just the same."

"He gave his three other wives an allowance."

"After he left them . . ."

He put the question crudely: "Did he act this way to prevent your giving money to Marco?"

She stared at him.

"I don't know. I didn't think of that. David never had any money on him either. It was Arnold who paid the bills at the end of the month. Now that I'm forty . . ."

She looked around as if to say that she would have to give all this up. The sallow creases at the corners of her nose deepened. She hesitated before getting up.

"If you'll excuse me one moment . . ."

She hurried into her bedroom and closed the door, and when she returned Maigret smelled another whiff of alcohol.

"What have you just been drinking?"

"A drop of whisky, if you must know. I'm dead on my feet. But sometimes I can last weeks without drinking."

"Except champagne?"

"Except a glass of champagne from time to time, that's true. But when I get into the state I'm in now, I need to . . ."

He could have sworn she had drunk straight from the bottle, greedily, the way some addicts inject themselves through their clothes to save time.

Her eyes were glittering more, her words came more volubly.

"I assure you I had not decided anything. I saw Marco with that woman and it gave me a jolt."

"Did you know her?"

"Yes. She's divorced, and her ex-husband, who's in the shipping business, had had dealings with David."

These people all knew one another, attended the same board meetings, met on the same beaches and at the same night clubs, and their wives apparently moved from one man's bed to another's with perfect abandon.

"I knew that she and Marco had had an affair at Deauville. I'd even been told she'd decided to marry him, but I hadn't believed it. . . . She's very rich and he doesn't have a penny."

"Did you decide to prevent that marriage?"

Her lips became a hard, thin line.

"Yes."

"Do you think Marco would have consented to it?"

Her eyes grew moist, but she held back the tears.

"I don't know. . . . I didn't think about it. I was watching them together. While he was dancing he intentionally went right past me without even a glance."

"So, logically, it's Marco who should have been killed?"

"What do you mean?"

"Didn't the thought of killing him ever occur to you? Didn't you ever threaten to do so?"

"How do you know that?"

"He didn't believe you'd be capable of it?"

"Did Van Meulen tell you that?"

"No."

"It wasn't as simple as that. . . . We had already had drinks before dinner. At the Monseigneur I finished off a bottle of champagne and I believe I took two or three sips from David's glass of whisky. I didn't know whether to make a scene, to go and drag Marco away from the arms of that horrible fat woman whose skin's as pink as a baby's . . .

"David insisted on our leaving. I finally followed him. In the car I didn't say a word. I planned to slip out of the hotel later on and go back to the night club to . . . I don't know what for. Don't ask me to make things clearer. . . . David must have guessed. . . . It was he who suggested that we have a nightcap in my rooms."

"Why in yours?"

The question surprised her and she repeated, in some bewilderment: "Why?"

She sought an answer, as though to satisfy herself.

"It was always David who came to mine . . . I think he didn't like . . . He had a thing about protecting his privacy."

"Did you tell him you intended to leave him?"

"I told him everything that was on my mind, that I was just a bitch, that I'd never be happy without Marco, that Marco had only to appear for me to . . ."

"What did David say?"

"He went on quietly drinking his whisky and looking at me with his big mischievous eyes. . . .

" 'What about money?' he finally objected. 'You know that Marco . . .' "

"Was the remark about Marco true?"

"Marco needs a lot of money. . . ."

"Hasn't it ever occurred to him to work?"

She gaped at him in astonishment, as if that question revealed boundless naïveté.

"What could he ever do? . . . Finally I got undressed . . ."

"Did anything happen between David and yourself?"

Again a look of surprise.

"Nothing ever happened. . . . You don't understand. . . . David had drunk a lot too, as he always did at bedtime."

"A third of a bottle?"

"Not quite. . . . I know why you're asking that. . . . It was I who drank a little whisky after he left, because I didn't feel well. I wanted to crumple up on my bed and stop thinking. I tried to sleep. Then I said to myself that it wouldn't work out with Marco, that it would never work out, and that it would be better if I died."

"How many pills did you take?"

"I don't know. . . . A whole handful . . . I felt better then. I was crying softly and beginning to fall asleep. Then I imagined my funeral, the cemetery and the . . . I began to struggle. I was afraid it was too late and that I wouldn't be able to call for help. I found I couldn't shout . . . the bell buttons seemed very far away . . . my arm was heavy. . . . You know, just as in dreams when you're trying to run away and your legs refuse to move. . . . I must have reached the bell button, since somebody did come."

She broke off on seeing Maigret's face, suddenly hard and stern.

"Why are you looking at me like that?"

"Why are you lying to me?"

He had almost been taken in.

"At what point did you go into the Colonel's room?"

"That's true. . . . I had forgotten. . . ."

She was shaking her head, really in tears now.

"Don't be hard on me. I swear I didn't mean to lie to you. . . The proof is that I told Jef Van Meulen the truth. . . .

Only when I found myself in hospital and was seized with panic did I first decide to pretend I didn't know what had happened. I was sure I wouldn't be believed, that I'd be suspected of killing David. . . . So now, when I was talking to you, I forgot that Van Meulen had advised me not to conceal anything."

"How long after the Colonel had left you did you go to his room?"

"Will you believe me now?"

"That depends."

"You see! It's always like that with me. . . . I do what I can. I have nothing to hide. Only I end up losing my head and I don't know what's happening to me. Can't I go have a drink, just one drop? I promise you I won't get drunk. . . . I can't stand it, Superintendent!"

He let her go, feeling almost inclined to ask for a drink himself.

"It was before swallowing the pills. . . . I hadn't decided to die yet, but I had already drunk the whisky. . . . I was tipsy and ill. . . . I felt sorry for what I'd said to David. . . . Life suddenly seemed terrifying. . . . I saw myself as a lonely old woman, without money, incapable of earning a living, since I've never learned to do anything. . . . David was my last chance. . . . When I left Van Meulen I was younger. . . . The proof is that . . ."

"That you found the Colonel after that."

She looked surprised and hurt by his aggressive manner.

"You can think what you like about me. *I* know, at any rate, how wrong you are. I was afraid of David's dropping me. I went in my nightgown, without even a robe, as far as his suite, and I found the door ajar."

"I asked you how much time had elapsed since the Colonel left you?"

"I don't know. I remember I smoked several cigarettes. They must have been found in the ashtray. David smoked only cigars."

"You saw nobody in his rooms?"

"Only him . . . I nearly screamed. I'm not sure I didn't scream."

"He was dead?"

She stared at him wide-eyed, as if the idea had struck her for the first time.

"He was . . . I think. In any case I thought so, and I ran away."

"Did you meet anyone in the hall?"

"No . . . But . . . wait a minute! . . . I heard the elevator going up. I'm sure of that, because I began running."

"Did you have any more to drink?"

"I may have . . . automatically. . . . Then I felt so depressed that I took the pills. I've told you the rest. . . . May I . . . ?"

She was no doubt going to ask his permission to take another drink of whisky, but the telephone rang, and she held out a shaky arm.

"Hello . . . Yes, he's here, yes."

It was restful, almost refreshing, to hear Lucas's voice, a calm, normal voice, and to imagine him sitting at his desk on Quai des Orfèvres.

"Is that you, Chief?"

"I was going to call you soon."

"I expected you to, but I thought I'd better bring you up to date at once. Marco Paverini is here."

"You found him?"

105

"It wasn't we who found him; he came on his own initiative. He showed up about twenty minutes ago, fit and well and quite unconcerned. He asked if you were here, and when he heard you weren't, he asked to speak to one of your colleagues. I saw him myself. For the moment I've left him with Janvier in your office."

"What does he say?"

"That he only learned about all this business through the papers."

"Last night?"

"Not till this morning. He was out of Paris, staying with some friends who have a country house in Nièvre and who were having a shooting party."

"Did the Dutch lady go with him?"

"To the shoot? Yes. They left together in her car. He claims they're going to get married. Her name is Anna de Groot and she's a divorcee."

"I know. . . . Go on."

Huddled in her armchair, the little Countess was listening to him, biting her nails, with their flaking varnish.

"I asked him what he'd been doing the night before."

"And?"

"He was in a night club, the Monseigneur."

"I know."

"With Anna de Groot."

"I know that, too."

"He saw the Colonel with his ex-wife."

"And then?"

"He went back with the Dutchwoman to her place."

"Where?"

"The George V, where she has a suite on the fourth floor."

106

"What time was this?"

"According to him, about half past three or four. I sent somebody to check it out, but I haven't had a reply yet. They went to bed and slept until ten the next morning. He claims they were invited over a week ago to this shooting party at the country house of a banker on Rue Auber. Marco Paverini left the George V and went home in a taxi to get his suitcase. He kept the taxi, which waited outside the door. He returned to the George V, and about half past eleven the two of them left in Anna de Groot's Jaguar. . . . This morning, just before leaving on the shoot, he glanced casually at the papers in the hall of the country house and immediately left for Paris, still in his shooting gear."

"Did the Dutchwoman come back with him?"

"No, she stayed behind. Lapointe called the country house to check and a manservant told him she had gone out shooting."

"What impression did he make on you?"

"He was perfectly at ease and seemed sincere. I thought he was really a nice guy."

Of course! They were all nice people!

"What should I do with him?"

"Send Lapointe to the George V. Let him investigate last night's comings and goings, and question the night staff. . . ."

"He'll have to visit their homes, because they're not on duty during the day."

"Let him do that. As for . . ."

He preferred not to mention the name in front of the woman, who had kept her eyes fixed on him.

"As for your visitor, you can't do anything at this juncture

107

but let him go. . . . Tell him not to leave Paris. Set somebody . . . Yes . . . Yes . . . The usual thing, you know! . . . I'll call you back later. I'm not alone."

Why did Maigret ask at the last minute: "What kind of weather are you having?"

"Sort of cool, with a little bright sunshine . . ."

As he hung up, the little Countess muttered, "Was it him?"

"Who?"

"Marco . . . You were talking about him, weren't you?"

"Are you sure you didn't meet him in the corridors of the George V or in the Colonel's rooms?"

She leaped out of her armchair in such a state of frenzy that he expected a fit of hysterics.

"I knew it!" she cried, her features distorted. "He was there with her, wasn't he, just above my head? . . . Yes! I know. . . . She always stays at the George V. . . . I found out where her rooms were. They were there together in bed."

She seemed beside herself with rage.

"They were there laughing and making love, while I . . ."

"Don't you think perhaps Marco was doing something else?"

"What?"

"Possibly holding the Colonel's head under the water?"

She could not believe her ears. Her body was quivering under the flimsy dressing gown, and she suddenly flung herself at Maigret, pounding him with her fists.

"Are you crazy? . . . Are you crazy? . . . How dare you? . . . You're a monster! . . . You . . ."

He felt ridiculous in that hotel room trying to grasp the

wrists of a fury whose energy was intensified tenfold by anger.

His tie askew, his hair disheveled, out of breath, he had finally succeeded in immobilizing her when there came a knock at the door.

*In which
Maigret is
invited out to lunch,
and learns some more
about VIPs*

The incident had ended less badly than might have been anticipated. For the little Countess, the knock on the door was providential, because it allowed her to extricate herself from a scene that she probably did not know how to bring to an end.

Once again she rushed into her bedroom, while the Superintendent, taking his time, rearranged his tie and smoothed his hair, and then opened the door into the hallway.

It was only the room waiter asking, with sudden diffidence, whether he might remove the breakfast tray. Had he been listening at the door, or without deliberately listening had he overheard the sounds of the scuffle? If so, he gave no indication of it, and when he left, the Countess reappeared looking calmer and wiping her lips.

"I suppose you intend to take me back to Paris?"

"Even if I wanted to I would have some pretty long formalities to go through."

"My lawyer here would not allow you to get an extradition order. But I want to go back myself, because I'm anxious to attend David's funeral. Are you taking the four-o'clock plane?"

"Probably, but you're not going to take it."

"And why not, may I ask?"

"Because I don't want to travel with you."

"I have a right to, don't I?"

Maigret was thinking of the journalists and photographers who would undoubtedly bombard her both in Geneva and at Orly.

"You may be within your rights, but if you try to take that plane I'll find some more or less legal means to stop you. I suppose you have no statement to make to me?"

The end of this interview had really been almost grotesque, and in order to recover contact with ordinary reality the Superintendent had followed it up with a telephone conversation of almost half an hour, with Lucas. The manager of the hotel had provided a small office near the reception desk on his own initiative.

Although Dr. Paul had not yet sent in his official report, he had given Lucas a preliminary report over the telephone. After the autopsy he was more than ever convinced that somebody had held David Ward down in his bathtub, because there could be no other explanation for the bruises on the shoulders. Furthermore, there were no signs of injury to the neck or back, such as would almost certainly have been noticeable had the Colonel met his death by slipping and hitting the rim of the tub.

Janvier had been shadowing Marco, and, as was to be expected, the first thing that the little Countess's ex-husband had done on leaving Quai des Orfèvres was to phone Anna de Groot.

Lucas had been pestered with endless calls, many of them from leading banks and financial companies.

"Are you coming back this afternoon, Chief?"

"On the four-o'clock plane."

Just as he was hanging up, he was handed an envelope that a uniformed policeman had brought for him. It was a charming note from the head of the Lausanne detective force, expressing his delight at having the opportunity to meet the famous Maigret at last, and inviting him to "a very simple lunch, in a quiet Vaudois inn on the lake."

Maigret, who had half an hour to wait, called Boulevard Richard-Lenoir.

"Are you still in Lausanne?" Madame Maigret asked.

On the previous day police headquarters had informed her of her husband's departure, and she had had news of him that morning through the papers.

"I'm catching a plane this afternoon, but that doesn't mean I'll be home early. Don't expect me for dinner."

"Are you bringing the Countess back?"

Of course she wasn't jealous, but for the first time Maigret thought he noticed a certain uneasiness, as well as the faintest trace of irony, in his wife's voice.

"I have no desire to bring her back."

"Oh!"

He lighted his pipe and left the hotel, informing the hall porter that if anyone asked for him, he would be back in a few minutes. Two photographers followed him, hoping that his actions would give something away.

He merely gazed into shopwindows, hands in pockets, and then entered a tobacconist's to buy a pipe, having left so hastily that he had only one with him, which was unusual.

He let himself be tempted by tins of various kinds of tobacco unknown in France, and bought three of different brands, then, as though seized with remorse, went into the next shop and bought for Madame Maigret a handkerchief embroidered with the arms of Lausanne.

The police chief picked him up at the appointed time. He was a big, athletically built man who must have been an avid skier.

"You don't mind if we go and eat out in the country, a few kilometers away? You don't have to worry about your plane. I'll have one of our cars drive you to the airport."

He was clear-skinned and so close-shaven that his cheeks shone. His whole appearance and bearing were those of a man who has remained in close contact with the countryside; as Maigret learned presently, his father was in fact a vine grower in the vicinity of Vevey.

They sat down in a lakeside inn where the only others present were a group of local people talking about the choral society to which they belonged.

"Will you allow me to choose the menu?"

He ordered dried meat from the Grisons, ham and country sausage, followed by salmon trout from the lake.

He kept watching Maigret with discreet, furtive glances that revealed his curiosity and admiration.

"She's a strange woman, isn't she?"

"The Countess?"

"Yes. She's well known here, too, because she spends part of the year in Lausanne."

He explained with a somewhat touching pride:

"We're a small country, Monsieur Maigret. But just because we're a small country, the proportion of VIPs is higher here than in Paris or even on the Riviera. You may have more of them than we do, but they are lost in the crowd. Here it's impossible not to notice them. They're the very same people who are seen on the Champs-Élysées and in Cannes on La Croisette."

Maigret was doing justice to the meal and to the light white wine that was served chilled in a misted carafe.

"We know Colonel Ward and practically all the people you're concerned with at the moment. By the way, Ward's third wife Muriel left in a hurry this morning for Paris."

"What sort of life does she lead in Lausanne?"

His companion had blue eyes that, when he was being thoughtful, grew lighter, almost transparent.

"That's not easy to explain. She has a comfortable apartment, fairly luxurious but not very large, in a new building at Ouchy. Her daughter, Ellen, is a boarder at a school where most of the students are American, English, Dutch, and German girls from wealthy families. We have many such schools in Switzerland; they send us children from all over the world."

"Yes, I know."

"Muriel Ward—I call her Ward because the divorce is not final yet and she still uses the name—belongs to what we call the club of unattached ladies. It's not a real club, of course. It has no regulations or dues or membership cards. It's the name we give to those ladies who come to live in Switzerland alone for various reasons. Some of them are divorced, others are widows. There are a few singers or famous music-hall stars, and some married women whose husbands come to visit them from time to time. They have their own reasons for being here, which don't concern us:

political or financial reasons, or sometimes reasons of health. We have royal highnesses and commoners, wealthy widows and women with modest incomes."

He related all this somewhat in the manner of a guide, with a slight smile that gave a touch of humor to his words.

"Their common characteristic is that they're all VIPs of some kind, whether because of their name or their wealth or what have you. And they form groups. It's not a club, but a set of groups more or less friendly or hostile to one another. Some of them rent rooms by the year at the Lausanne-Palace, which you have seen. The richest of them have villas at Ouchy or country houses in the area. They give tea parties for each other or meet at concerts. . . . But isn't it just the same in Paris? The difference, as I was saying, is that here you notice them more. . . . We get men, too, from all over the place, who have decided to live year-round or part of the year in Switzerland. . . . I mentioned the Lausanne-Palace—well, right now there are about twenty members of King Saud's family living there. Add to that delegates to the international conferences, UNESCO and so forth, which take place in our country, and you'll understand how busy we are. Our police work discreetly, but, I like to think, efficiently. . . . If I can be of any help to you . . ."

Maigret was smiling in much the same way as his host. He realized that although Swiss hospitality was generous, the police were nonetheless well informed as to the doings of all these well-known personalities.

What he had just been told, in fact, amounted to, "If you have any questions to ask . . ."

He said softly, "I gather Ward was on excellent terms with his ex-wives."

"Why should he have held any grudges? It was he who left them when he was tired of them."

"Did he treat them generously?"

"Not excessively. He gave them a decent allowance, but not a lavish one."

"What sort of person is Muriel Halligan?"

"An American woman."

He put a great deal of meaning into the words.

"I don't know why the Colonel chose to get his divorce in Switzerland . . . unless he had other reasons for staying here. The fact is that the proceedings have been dragging on for two years. Muriel has chosen the two best lawyers in this country and she must know what that'll cost here. Her plea, which apparently has been upheld in certain American courts, is that since her husband has accustomed her to a certain standard of living he must enable her to maintain it to the end of her days."

"And the Colonel didn't accept that?"

"He has excellent lawyers, too. On three or four occasions there was a rumor that a settlement had been reached, but I don't think the final documents have been signed."

"I suppose that while the case is *sub judice* the wife is careful to avoid any indiscretions?"

The Lausanne policeman filled their glasses with deliberate slowness, as if seeking to weigh his words.

"No indiscretions, no. . . . The ladies of the club generally don't go in for anything sensational. . . . I suppose you've met John Arnold?"

"He showed up at the George V before anybody else."

"He's a bachelor," the policeman remarked laconically.

"And . . .?"

117

"At one time it was whispered that he was gay. I know from the staff of the hotels where he stays that this is not the case."

"What else do you know?"

"He was and always had been a close friend of the Colonel's. He was his confidant, his secretary, and his business agent all rolled into one. Besides his legal wives, the Colonel used to have passing affairs, generally brief ones, sometimes for a night or just an hour. Since he was too lazy to court women properly and since, in his position, he found it embarrassing to make propositions to a cabaret dancer or a flower girl, John Arnold arranged things for him."

"I see what you mean."

"Then you can guess the rest. Arnold took his commission in kind. I've heard, although I have no formal proof, that he also did so with Ward's legal wives."

"Muriel?"

"He's come twice to Lausanne to see her alone but there's nothing to prove that he wasn't acting in Ward's behalf."

"The Countess?"

"Undoubtedly! And he wasn't the only one. When she's had enough champagne to drink she often feels the need to pour out her heart to somebody."

"Did Ward know?"

"I haven't had much to do with Colonel Ward. You forget that I'm just a policeman.

They both smiled. It was a strange conversation, with unspoken implications and many innuendoes that they both understood.

"As I see it, Ward knew a lot but didn't mind very much.

In Monte Carlo, as I see from this morning's papers, you met another customer of ours, Monsieur Van Meulen. . . . The two men, who were great friends, had seen too much of life to expect from people, particularly from women, more than they were likely to get. . . . They were roughly of the same caliber, except that Van Meulen is cooler and has more self-control, whereas the Colonel had a weakness for liquor. . . . I imagine you'll want coffee?"

Maigret was long to remember that lunch in the little restaurant that reminded him of a certain *guinguette* on the banks of the Marne, with Swiss decorum added—less lively, perhaps, but more genuinely intimate.

"Will the Countess take the same plane as you?"

"I told her she can't."

"It'll depend on what she has to drink between now and four o'clock. You'd rather she didn't take it?"

"She's a little too conspicuous, and hard to take."

"She won't be on it," the chief promised. "Would it be a bore for you to stop by for a few minutes at our office? My men are so anxious to meet you . . ."

They did him the honors of their police headquarters, which was in a new building on the same floor as a private bank and just below a ladies' hairdresser. Maigret shook hands, smiled, repeated the same friendly remarks ten times over, feeling euphoric from the light Vaudois wine.

"It's high time I put you in your car. If you wait any longer we'll have to have the siren going all the way."

He was soon back in the atmosphere of air terminals, loud-speakers, bars where uniformed pilots and stewardesses drank hurried cups of coffee.

119

Then came the plane ride over mountains that were lower than those he had seen that morning, and meadows and farms glimpsed between clouds.

Lapointe was waiting at Orly with one of the black police cars.

"Have a good trip, Chief?"

He was back in the suburbs of Paris, where a fine afternoon was just ending.

"Haven't you had any rain?"

"Not a drop. I thought you'd want me to meet you."

"Anything new?"

"I haven't heard all the latest. Lucas has been co-ordinating information. I went to see some of the night staff, which meant a lot of traveling, since most of them live in the suburbs."

"What did you find out?"

"Nothing definite. I tried to reconstruct a schedule with the times everyone arrived and left. It's not easy. Apparently there are three hundred and ten guests in the hotel and they all keep coming and going, telephoning, ringing for the waiter or the chambermaid, wanting a taxi, a messenger, the manicurist, Lord knows what. Furthermore, the staff are afraid of talking too much. Most of them give evasive answers."

As he drove, he pulled a piece of paper out of his pocket and gave it to Maigret.

8 P.M. *The chambermaid on the third floor goes into number 332, the Countess's suite, and finds her in her dressing gown having a manicure.*

"*Have you come to prepare the bed, Annette?*"

"*Yes*, Madame la Comtesse."

"*Will you come back in half an hour?*"

*8:10 P.M. Colonel Ward at the hotel bar with John Arnold. The Colonel looks at his watch, leaves his companion, and goes up to his suite. Arnold orders a sandwich.*

*8:22 P.M. The Colonel, from his suite, asks for a call to be put through to Cambridge and speaks to his son for about ten minutes. It seems he used to call him like this twice a week, always at about the same time.*

*8·30 P.M. or thereabouts. At the bar, Arnold goes into the phone booth. He must have made a call to a Paris number, because the switchboard girl made no note of it.*

*8:45 P.M. The Colonel calls number 332 from his own suite, probably to find out if the Countess is ready.*

*About 9 P.M. The Colonel and the Countess emerge from the elevator and hand in their keys on the way out. The doorman calls a taxi for them. Ward gives the address of a restaurant near the Madeleine.*

Lapointe watched Maigret as he read.

"I went to the restaurant," he explained. "Nothing special there. They often dine there and they're always given the same table. Three or four people came to shake hands with the Colonel. There were no signs of a quarrel between our two. While the Countess was eating her dessert the Colonel, who never has dessert, lighted a cigar and looked through the evening papers."

*11:30 P.M. The couple arrives at the Monseigneur.*

"There, again, they're habitués," said Lapointe, "and the

gipsy band automatically strikes up a special tune as soon as the Countess appears. Champagne and whisky. The Colonel never dances."

Maigret imagined the Colonel, first at the restaurant taking advantage of the fact that he never had dessert to read his newspaper, and then sitting on the red-velvet seats of the Monseigneur. He did not dance and he would not have flirted, since he and his companion were old acquaintances. The musicians would come up and play at his table.

"There, again, they're habitués," Lapointe had said.

Three nights, four nights a week? And elsewhere, in London or Rome, at Cannes or Lausanne, he must presumably have frequented almost identical night clubs, where they played the same tune on the Countess's appearance and where, again, he did not dance.

He had an eighteen-year-old son at Cambridge to whom he spoke over the telephone for a few minutes every three days, and a daughter in Switzerland whom, presumably, he also called.

He had had three wives, the first of whom had remarried and led the same kind of life as he, then Alice Perrin, who divided her time between London and Paris, and finally Muriel Halligan, who belonged to the unattached ladies' club.

In the streets, people on their way home from work were hurrying toward métro stations and busstops.

"We're there, Chief."

"I know."

It was rather dark already in the courtyard of police headquarters, and the lights were on in the perennially dingy staircase.

He did not go directly to see Lucas, but went into his office, switched on the light, and took his usual seat, with Lapointe's notebook in front of him.

*12:15 P.M. Ward receives telephone call. I couldn't find out where it came from.*

Automatically, it seemed, Maigret reached out for his own receiver.

"Put me through to my home number. . . . Hello, is that you? . . . I'm back. . . . Yes, I'm in my office. . . . I don't know yet. . . . Everything's all right. . . . No, no! I assure you. . . . Why should I be feeling depressed?"

What reason had his wife to ask him that question? He had just wanted to get in touch with her, that was all.

*About 12:30 A.M. Marco Paverini and Anna de Groot arrive at the Monseigneur.*

(NOTE: *Anna de Groot had left the George V at 7 P.M. She was alone. She met Marco at Fouquet's, where they dined hastily before going to the theater. Neither of them in evening dress. At Fouquet's, as at the Monseigneur, they are well known and their liaison seems accepted as official.*)

Maigret was aware of the number of journeys this report represented and of the patient efforts Lapointe had made in order to obtain such ostensibly unimportant information.

*12:55 P.M. The bartender at the George V informs his five or six remaining customers that he is going to close. John Arnold buys a Havana and goes into the lobby, taking with him the three men with whom he was playing cards.*

(NOTE: *I have not been able to ascertain whether Arnold*

*left the bar during the evening. The bartender cannot say categorically. Until 10 P.M. all the tables and all the stools were occupied. The bartender then noticed Arnold in the left-hand corner by the window in the company of three newly arrived Americans, who included a film producer and an actor's agent. They were playing poker. I could not find out, either, whether Arnold knew them already or had just met them that evening in the bar. They were using chips, but by the end the bartender noticed dollars changing hands. He thinks they were playing for high stakes. He does not know which of them won.)*

1:10 A.M. *The waiter is summoned to the little Empire-style lounge at the end of the lobby and asked if refreshments are still obtainable. He answers affirmatively and is told to bring a bottle of whisky, soda, and four glasses. The four customers from the bar had found this place to continue their game.*

1:55 A.M. *On returning to the Empire-style lounge, the waiter finds it deserted. The bottle is almost empty, the chips on the table, and cigar butts in an ashtray.*

*(I questioned the night concierge on this subject. The producer's name is Mark P. Jones, and he has come over to France with a famous American comedian to make a film, or some sequences of a film, in the south of France. The star's agent's name is Art Levinson. The concierge does not know who the third player was. He has seen him several times in the lobby, but the man is not a hotel guest. He thinks he saw him leave that night about 2 A.M. I asked him if Arnold was with the man. He couldn't answer one way or the other. He had been on the telephone, a fifth-floor guest was complaining of the noise her neighbors were making; he went up*

124

*himself to request the couple in question, tactfully, to be less exuberant.*)

Maigret leaned back in his chair, slowly filled his pipe, and looked at the evening grayness outside his windows.

*About 2:05 A.M. The Colonel and the Countess leave the Monseigneur, take a taxi that was standing outside the night club, and drive back to the George V. I easily traced the taxi. The couple did not exchange a word throughout the journey.*

*2:15 A.M. The room waiter summoned to number 332. Finds the Colonel sitting in an armchair, looking tired, as he usually did at that time of night, and the Countess, opposite him, taking off her shoes and massaging her feet. She orders a bottle of champagne and one of whisky.*

*About 3 A.M. Anna de Groot returns to the hotel, accompanied by Marco Paverini. Both cheerful and affectionate, but discreetly so. She seems a little livelier than he, presumably excited by champagne. They are speaking English together, although both speak French fluently, the Dutchwoman with a noticeable accent. They go up on the elevator. A few minutes later they ring for mineral water.*

*3:35 A.M. A call from number 332. The Countess tells the operator that she is dying and asks for a doctor. The operator first summons the nurse and then calls Dr. Frère.*

Maigret ran through the rest more rapidly, then got up and opened the door of the inspectors' room. He found Lucas on the telephone beside his green-shaded lamp.

"I don't understand," Lucas was shouting in exasperation. "I tell you, I don't understand a word you're saying. . . . I don't even know what language you're speaking. . . . No, I don't have an interpreter on hand. . . ."

He hung up and mopped his brow.

"As far as I could tell, that was a call from Copenhagen. I don't know if they were speaking German or Danish. . . . It's been going on ever since this morning. Everybody's clamoring for details."

He stood up apologetically.

"I'm sorry, I haven't even asked you if you had a good trip. In fact, I took a call for you from Lausanne . . . to say that the Countess is taking the night train and will arrive in Paris at seven in the morning."

"Did she make the call herself?"

"No. The person you had lunch with . . ."

That was kind, and Maigret appreciated the tactfulness of the gesture. A favor, discreetly done . . . The police chief had not given his name. Actually, Maigret, having lost his card, had already forgotten it.

"What did Arnold do today?" he asked.

"First of all, this morning, he went to a hotel in the Faubourg Saint-Honoré, the Bristol, where the English solicitor Philps is staying."

The Englishman had not gone to the George V, too cosmopolitan for his liking, or to the Scribe, which was too French, but had chosen to stay opposite the British Embassy, as though he didn't want to feel too remote from his own country.

"They conferred for an hour, then they went to an American bank on Avenue de l'Opéra, then to a British bank on Place Vendôme, in both of which they were immediately received by the manager. They stayed there for a considerable

126

time. At noon exactly they separated on the sidewalk of Place Vendôme, and the solicitor took a taxi back to his hotel, where he had lunch by himself."

"And Arnold?"

"He went through the Tuileries Gardens on foot without hurrying, as if he had plenty of time to spare, occasionally looking at his watch to make sure. He even browsed a little in the bookstalls along the Seine, glancing at old books and engravings, and at a quarter to one he went into the Hotel des Grands Augustins. He was soon joined by Ward's third wife."

"Muriel Halligan?"

"Yes. She usually stays at that hotel. It seems she arrived at Orly about half past eleven, and had taken a bath and rested for half an hour before going down to the bar."

"Did she make any calls?"

"No."

So she must have called from Lausanne before leaving, to make her date with Arnold.

"Did they have lunch together?"

"In a little restaurant on Rue Jacob which looks like a *bistrot* but is very expensive. Torrence, who followed them in, says the food is marvelous but the prices are steep. They chatted quietly like old friends, but spoke too low for Torrence to catch a word. Then Arnold took her back to her hotel and left in a taxi to meet Philps. At the Bristol there have been endless telephone calls, from London, Cambridge, Amsterdam, Lausanne. A number of people have visited Philps in his suite, including a Parisian lawyer, Demonteau, who stayed longer than the rest. There's a group of journalists in the lobby. They're waiting to know when the funeral

127

will be and whether it will be in London, Paris, or Lausanne. It seems that Ward's official residence was Lausanne. They're also anxious to know about the will, but until now they've received no information at all. . . . Furthermore, the reporters claim that Ward's two children are expected any minute. . . . You look tired, Chief."

"No . . . I don't know."

He was feeling more limp than usual and would have found it hard to say what he was thinking about. He was experiencing the same sensation as after a sea crossing; his body still felt as if it were in the plane, while images mingled confusedly in his mind. It had all happened too fast: too many people, too many things one after the other. Joseph Van Meulen lying naked on his bed, in the hands of his masseur, and then leaving Maigret in the lobby of the Hotel de Paris to go out, wearing a dinner jacket, to the gala at the Sporting Club . . . The little Countess, with her tired face and the creases beside her nose and her unsteady, tippler's hands . . . And then the fair-haired Lausanne police chief . . . whatever his name was . . . who had filled his glass with light cool wine while smiling openly, and with a touch of irony, at the people he talked about . . . And the "club of unattached ladies" . . .

Now, in addition, there was that four-handed poker party in the bar of the George V, and subsequently in the Empire-style lounge. . . .

And Philps in his English hotel opposite the British Embassy, and those attentive bank managers . . . Conversations, telephone calls, the French lawyer Demonteau, the journalists in the lobby of the Faubourg Saint-Honoré hotel and at the door of the George V, even though there was nothing more to be seen there . . .

A boy at Cambridge who would probably be a multimillionaire himself had suddenly learned that his father, who had phoned him the day before from a continental hotel, was dead.

And a fourteen-year-old girl whom her schoolmates may have envied because she was packing her bags to go to her father's funeral . . .

At that very moment the little Countess was probably tipsy, but she would nonetheless catch the night train. Whenever she felt faint she just had to take one more drink to pull herself together. Until she fell apart for good.

"You look as if you just got an idea, Chief?"

"Do I?"

He shrugged his shoulders in a disillusioned way. Then he asked, in his turn:

"Are you very tired?"

"Not too bad."

"In that case, let's go out for a quiet meal together at the Brasserie Dauphine."

The company there would be different from that at the George V or on the airplane, or at Monte Carlo or Lausanne. A heavy smell of cooking, like that of a country inn. The wife at her stove, the husband behind the counter, the daughter helping the waiter serve.

"And after that?"

"After that I'm going to start all over again, as if I knew nothing, as if I'd never met any of these people."

"Shall I go with you?"

"It's not worth while. To do this job, I'd just as soon be alone. . . ."

Lucas knew what that meant. Maigret was going to prowl around Avenue George V, brooding, puffing on his pipe, glancing briefly left and right, sitting down occasionally and getting up again almost at once, as if he didn't know what to do with his big body.

And nobody, not even Maigret himself, could say how long it would go on, and the prospect was not a pleasant one.

Someone who had seen him behaving thus one day had commented disrespectfully:

"He looks like a huge sick animal!"

*In which
Maigret is made
to feel unwanted,
and indeed is regarded
with suspicion*

He took the métro because he had plenty of time and didn't plan to travel far that night. He seemed to have overeaten deliberately so as to feel even more cumbrous. When he left Lucas on Place Dauphine, the latter had hesitated briefly, opening his mouth to say something, and the superintendent had looked at him expectantly.

"No . . . It's nothing . . .," Lucas had decided.

"Tell me. . . ."

"I was going to ask you whether it's worth while for me to go to bed. . . ." Because when the chief was in this particular mood, it usually meant that before very long the last act would be played out within the four walls of his office.

As chance would have it, this almost always took place at night, with the rest of the building in darkness, and several of them would take turns staying with the man or woman who had gone into police headquarters as a mere suspect but would leave it, after a certain length of time, wearing handcuffs.

Maigret knew what was on Lucas's mind. Without being

superstitious, he was reluctant to anticipate events, and at such moments he never felt self-confident.

"You go to bed."

He felt a little chilly. He had left home the morning of the previous day sure of returning to Boulevard Richard-Lenoir at noon for lunch. Was it only the day before? It seemed to him that all this had begun much longer ago.

He emerged from underground onto the Champs-Élysées, where the avenue was ablaze with lights and the fall evening was mild enough for the café terraces to be crowded with people. His hands in his jacket pockets, he walked down Avenue George V, where, in front of the hotel, a giant in uniform stared at him in surprise as he pushed the revolving door.

This was the night doorman. On his previous visit, Maigret had seen the day staff. The doorman obviously wondered what this sullen-faced man in the travel-crumpled suit who was not a hotel guest was up to.

The bellboy on duty on the other side of the revolving door displayed equal curiosity and surprise, and was on the point of asking Maigret what he wanted.

Some twenty people were scattered around the lobby, most of them in dinner jackets or evening dress; diamonds and mink were displayed, and, as Maigret moved forward, he encountered a succession of scents.

Since the bellboy was staring fixedly at him, ready to pursue and accost him if he ventured too far, Maigret chose to go straight to the reception desk, where the attendants, in their black morning coats, were all unfamiliar to him.

"Is Monsieur Gilles in his office?"

"He's at home. What do you want?"

He had often noticed that the night staff in hotels are less obliging than those on day duty. Almost invariably one has the impression that they are an inferior grade of personnel who bear the world a grudge for making them live the wrong way around, working while other people sleep.

"I'm Superintendent Maigret," he murmured.

"Do you want to go upstairs?"

"I'll probably go up. . . . I might just as well warn you that I intend to be around in the hotel for a while. Don't worry. I'll be as discreet as possible."

"The keys of 332 and 347 aren't at the concierge's desk. I have them here. We left the rooms just as they were, at the request of the examining magistrate."

"I know."

He thrust the keys into his pocket and, encumbered with his hat, looked around for somewhere to put it. Finally he laid it on one armchair and sat down in another, looking like any number of other people waiting in the lobby.

From where he sat he could see the reception clerk pick up the telephone, and he realized that it was to inform the manager of his visit. The proof of this was that a few minutes later the tail-coated clerk came up to him.

"I've got Monsieur Gilles on the line. I'm instructing the staff to let you come and go as you please. However, Monsieur Gilles would like to remind you . . ."

"I know! I know. . . . Does Monsieur Gilles live in the hotel?"

"No. He has a house at Sèvres."

To interrogate the night concierge, Lapointe had had to go as far as Joinville. The bartender, as Maigret knew, lived even farther from Paris, in the Chevreuse Valley, where he kept chickens and ducks, and had a big kitchen garden that he cultivated himself.

It was a little paradoxical! Guests paid astronomical prices to sleep a stone's throw from the Champs-Élysées, while the staff—at least those who could afford such genuine luxury —fled to the countryside as soon as their work was done.

The groups standing around, particularly those in evening dress, were people who had not yet dined, and who were waiting until their parties were complete to go off to Maxim's, La Tour d'Argent, or some other restaurant of the same caliber. There were some of them at the bar, too, having a final cocktail before starting on what, to them, was the most important part of the day: dinner and the hours after dinner.

The same scene, with the same cast, must have been played in exactly the same way on the previous night. At her stall, the florist was making up corsages. The theater-ticket agent was handing tickets to late-comers. The concierge was suggesting night clubs to people who did not yet know where to go.

Maigret had intentionally taken a Calvados after his meal out of sheer contrariness, because he was about to re-enter a world where one did not drink Calvados, much less marc, but only whisky, champagne, or Napoléon brandy.

A group of South Americans cheered loudly as a young woman in a blond mink coat came sweeping out of one of the elevators to make a star's entrance.

Was she pretty? The little Countess, as he'd been told, was wonderful; but he had seen her up close, without any makeup, had even caught her drinking whisky from the bottle, like a down-and-out alcoholic swigging red wine.

Why, during the last few minutes, had he felt as if he were living on board a ship? The atmosphere of the hotel lobby reminded him of that trip he had made to the United States when an American multimillionaire (another one!) had begged him to come over and solve a thorny problem. He remembered the confidences imparted by the purser one night when they had been left alone in the saloon after the somewhat puerile games that had been organized there.

"Did you know, Superintendent, that in first class there are three staff to serve a single passenger?"

And, indeed, every twenty yards or so on decks, in lounges or gangways, one met a member of the staff, uniformed or white-jacketed, ready to oblige in some way or other.

Here, too. In the bedrooms there were three bell buttons marked HOUSE STEWARD, CHAMBERMAID, ROOM WAITER, and alongside each—couldn't some of the guests read?—the silhouette of the appropriate domestic.

At the entrance, in the yellowish light over the sidewalk, two or three doormen and car attendants, not to mention porters in green aprons, were standing at attention as if at the doors of a barracks; and in every corner more men in uniform stood waiting, bolt upright, with faraway looks in their eyes.

"Believe it or not," the purser had continued, "the hardest part of our job on the ship isn't keeping the engines running, steering the vessel, navigating in heavy weather, or arriving on time in New York or Le Havre. Nor is it feeding a population as large as that of an arrondissement, or keeping cabins and lounges in order. What gives us the most trouble is . . ." He had paused a moment. "Is *keeping the passengers en-*

137

*tertained.* We have to find diversions for them from the minute they get up until the minute they go to bed, and some of them don't go to bed before dawn. . . ."

That was why they started serving bouillon on board as soon as breakfast was over. And then games began, and cocktails. . . . Then came caviar, *foie gras,* duck *à l'orange,* and *omelettes flambées.*

"Most of them are people who have seen everything, who've enjoyed themselves in every conceivable way, and yet we must at all costs . . ."

To keep himself from dozing off, Maigret got up and went to look for the Empire-style lounge, which he discovered eventually, dimly lit and solemn and deserted now, except for an old white-haired gentleman in a dinner jacket asleep in an armchair, his open mouth still holding a cigar that had gone out. Farther along he came to the dining room, and the headwaiter on guard at the door looked him over from head to foot. He did not offer Maigret a table; had he realized that this was not an authentic guest?

In spite of the man's censorious expression, Maigret cast a glance into the room where, under the lighted chandeliers, about a dozen tables were occupied.

An idea, although not a particularly original one, was taking shape in his mind. He went past an elevator beside which was stationed a fair young man in olive-green livery. This was not the same elevator he had taken with the manager on the previous morning. And he discovered yet a third in another location.

He was being watched. The chief reception clerk probably hadn't had time to inform the whole staff, but had merely alerted the heads of the various departments to his presence.

Nobody asked him what he wanted, what he was looking for, where he was going, but no sooner was he out of the range of one set of suspicious eyes than he found himself under equally intense scrutiny by another.

His inspiration . . . It had not yet taken clear shape, but still he had the feeling he had made an important discovery. It was roughly this: certainly all these people—and he included the guests of the George V and those of the Monte Carlo and Lausanne hotels, the Wards and Van Meulens and Countess Paverinis, all those who lead that kind of life —would feel lost, defenseless, naked, as it were, as helpless and clumsy and frail as babies, if they were suddenly plunged into ordinary life.

Would they be capable of elbowing their way through a crowd to take the métro, consulting a train schedule, asking for a ticket at the ticket counter, carrying a suitcase?

In this world, from the moment they left their hotel suites until they were settled in identical rooms in New York, London, or Lausanne, they never had to worry about their luggage, which was automatically passed from hand to unseen hand; later, they would find their belongings put away for them in the proper places. . . . They themselves were passed from hand to hand. . . .

What was it Van Meulen had said about *interest providing an adequate motive*? Could someone kill from self-interest?

Maigret was becoming aware that the amount of money involved was relatively unimportant. He was even beginning to understand those American divorcees who insist on being maintained for the rest of their lives in the style to which their ex-husbands had accustomed them.

He could hardly picture the little Countess going into a *bistrot*, ordering a cup of coffee, and coping with a pay phone.

This was a secondary point, of course. . . . But aren't these secondary points often the most important? Living in an apartment, would Louise Paverini be capable of regulating the heat, lighting the gas stove in the kitchen, and boiling herself an egg?

His thoughts were more complicated than this, so complicated that he could not define them clearly.

How many people were there throughout the world who went from one place to another sure of encountering the same atmosphere everywhere, the same attentive service, practically the same people looking after the petty details of life for them?

A few thousand, probably. The purser on the *Liberté* had told him: "you can't invent anything fresh to amuse them with, because they like to stick to their habits. . . ."

Just as they liked to stick to the same setting, barring a few details. Was this a means of reassuring themselves, of deluding themselves that they were at home? Even the mirrors and tie hangers in the bedrooms were in identical positions.

"It's no use entering our profession unless you have a good memory for names and faces."

It was not the ship's purser who had said this, but the concierge of a hotel on the Champs-Élysées where Maigret had made some investigations twenty years earlier.

"Our guests insist on being recognized, even if they've only been here once before."

Probably that, too, gave them some kind of reassurance. Little by little Maigret had come to feel less severely critical of them. It seemed as if they were afraid of something, afraid of themselves, of reality, of solitude. They moved in a limited circle, among a few places in which they could be sure of being treated with the same care and consideration, of eating the same dishes and drinking the same champagne or the same whisky.

Maybe it wasn't even that they enjoyed it so much, but just that once they acquired the habit they were incapable of living in any other way.

Was this an adequate motive? Maigret had begun to think so, and consequently the death of Colonel Ward appeared in a fresh light.

Someone in his circle had been threatened, or felt threatened, with suddenly having to live like everybody else, and had lacked the courage to do so.

Moreover, Ward's death must have enabled that person to keep up the way of life that he or she could not bear to renounce.

Nothing was known about the will. Maigret had not heard to which lawyer it had been entrusted. John Arnold had implied that there might have been several wills placed in the hands of different lawyers.

Was Maigret perhaps wasting his time prowling the corridors of the George V? Wouldn't it be more sensible to go to bed and wait?

He went into the bar. The bartender on night duty didn't know him, either, but one of the waiters recognized him from his photographs and whispered something to his boss, who frowned, seeming uneasy rather than flattered at the prospect of serving Superintendent Maigret.

There were many people there, and the air was thick with cigar and cigarette smoke; besides the superintendent's, there was only one other pipe smoker.

"What can I give you?"

"Do you have any Calvados?"

He didn't see any on the shelves, where every brand of whisky was displayed. The barman unearthed a bottle, however, and filled a huge balloon-shaped glass, as if any other sort of vessel for liquor was unknown here.

For the most part, people were speaking English. Maigret recognized one woman, a mink stole casually thrown over her shoulders, with whom he had dealt at police headquarters in the days when she worked for a petty Corsican pimp in Montmartre.

That was two years ago. She had wasted no time, for she now wore a diamond ring and a diamond bracelet. She condescended to recognize the policeman, however, and fluttered her eyelashes at him discreetly.

Three men were sitting around a table at the far end of the room, on the left near the silk-curtained windows, and Maigret asked on the off-chance: "Isn't that Mark Jones, the producer?"

"The short fat guy, yes . . ."

"Which one is Art Levinson?"

"The dark-haired one in the horn-rimmed glasses."

"Who's the third?"

"I've seen him several times, but I don't know who he is."

The bartender answered reluctantly, as though he disliked having to give away his customers.

"What do I owe you?"

"Don't worry about it. . . ."

"I'd like to pay."

"Have it your way. . . ."

Without using the elevator, he went slowly upstairs to the third floor, musing that not many guests must tread on that red-carpeted stair. He met a woman in black with a notebook in her hand and a pencil behind her ear, some member of the hotel hierarchy; he assumed from the bunch of keys at her waist that she was responsible for giving orders to the chambermaids on certain floors and distributing sheets and towels.

She turned to look at him, appearing to hesitate, and probably informed the management that an odd-looking individual was wandering around the back regions of the George V.

For he had unintentionally strayed into the back regions. He had pushed open the door through which the woman had emerged and discovered another staircase, narrower and uncarpeted. Its walls were dingier. A half-open door disclosed a closet full of brooms with a huge pile of dirty linen in the middle.

There was no one around. Nor was there anyone on the floor above in another, more spacious room that contained a card table and chairs. There was a tray on the table with plates—cutlet bones and sauce and a few congealed fried potatoes.

Above the door he saw a set of bells, with three electric-light bulbs of different colors.

He saw many things in the course of an hour, met a few people, waiters and chambermaids, a shoeshine boy cleaning shoes. Most of them looked at him in surprise, or stared after him mistrustfully. But with one exception nobody spoke a word to him.

Maybe they thought that since he was there he must have the right to be there. Or did they hastily call the manager as soon as his back was turned?

He met a workman in overalls carrying tools that suggested plumbing trouble somewhere or other. The man, who had a cigarette stuck to his lip, looked him up and down and asked: "Are you looking for something?"

"No, thanks anyway."

The man moved off shrugging his shoulders, turned around once again, and finally disappeared behind a door.

Maigret was not interested in revisiting the two suites he already knew; he went up above the third floor, to see the lay of the land. He had learned to recognize the doors that divided the corridors with their spotless walls and thick carpets from the less luxurious back passages and narrow stairways.

Passing from one side to the other, noticing here a freight elevator, there a waiter asleep on his chair or two chambermaids telling one another about their illnesses, he eventually emerged onto the roof, surprised at suddenly seeing stars overhead and the colored halo of the Champs-Élysées glowing in the sky.

He stopped there for a little while, emptying his pipe, walking around the flat roof, leaning over the balustrade from time to time, watching the cars glide noiselessly along

the avenue, pull up in front of the hotel, and drive off again
with their load of richly dressed women and gentlemen in
black and white.

Across the street, Rue François Ier was brightly lighted
up, and the English pharmacy at its intersection with Avenue George V was still open. Was it open unusually late, or
did it have regular evening hours? With the customers from
the George V and those from the Prince de Galles next door,
who fussed over their health and turned night into day, it
must do good business.

On the left, Rue Christophe Colomb, which was quieter,
was lighted only by the red neon light of a restaurant or
nightclub, and large gleaming cars stood idle along both
curbs.

Farther back, in Rue Magellan, was a bar, the kind of *bistrot* frequented by chauffeurs in rich quarters. A man in a
white jacket, probably a waiter, crossed the street and went
in.

Maigret's mind was working slowly, and it took him some
time to find the way down again from the roof. Later on he
strayed into a room where a headwaiter was finishing up the
contents of someone's tray.

When he reappeared in the bar it was eleven o'clock and
there were fewer people drinking. The three Americans he
had noticed earlier were still in the same place playing poker,
together with a fourth, another American, a huge gaunt
fellow.

This man's high-heeled shoes puzzled the superintendent
at first, until he realized that they were actually cowboy
boots, the multicolored leather legs of which were concealed

by his trousers. A man from Texas or Arizona; he was more demonstrative than the others and spoke in a loud voice. One expected to see him pull a revolver from his belt.

Maigret eventually sat down on a stool and the bartender asked: "The same?"

He nodded, and then asked: "Do you know him?"

"I don't know his name, but he owns a lot of oil wells. Apparently the pumps work by themselves and this man makes a million a day without doing a thing."

"Was he here the night before last?"

"No. He arrived this morning. He's leaving tomorrow for Cairo and Saudi Arabia, where he has interests."

"Were the three others here?"

"Yes."

"With Arnold?"

"Wait a minute. . . . The night before last . . . Yes . . . One of your inspectors has already asked me about that."

"I know. . . . Who's the third, the one with fair hair?"

"I don't know his name. He's not staying at the hotel. I think he's at the Crillon and I've heard he owns a chain of restaurants."

"Does he speak French?"

"None of them do, except Mr. Levinson, who lived in Paris before he became a theatrical agent. . . ."

"Do you know what he used to do?"

The bartender shrugged his shoulders.

"Would you go and ask the one who's staying at the Crillon a question for me?"

The bartender made a face, but, not daring to refuse, he asked without enthusiasm: "What question?"

"I'd like to know where he and Arnold separated after they left the George V yesterday."

The bartender, preparing his smile, went across to the four poker players' table. He leaned over toward the third man, who stared at Maigret with some curiosity, and the other three followed suit, having learned who he was. The explanation took longer than might have been expected.

At last the bartender returned, while the game was resumed in the left-hand corner of the room.

"He asked me why you needed to know, and pointed out that in his country things aren't done this way. . . . He couldn't remember right away. He had a lot to drink the night before last. He'll be like that again when we close tonight. They continued their game in the Empire Room."

"Yes, I know that."

"He lost ten thousand dollars, but he's making up for it now."

"Did Arnold win?"

"I didn't ask him that. He thinks he remembers that they shook hands at the door of the Empire Room. . . . He says he thought that Arnold, whom he met only a few days ago, was staying at the George V."

Maigret showed no reaction. He spent a good quarter of an hour over his drink, casually watching the poker players. The young woman he had recognized was no longer there, but there was another, alone, whose diamonds were fake and who seemed to take as avid an interest in the game as he did.

Maigret directed the bartender's attention to her with a glance.

"I thought you didn't allow that type. . . ."

"Theoretically, no. We make an exception for two or three that we know, who can be trusted to behave themselves. It's almost a necessity. Otherwise, guests go and pick up girls in the street and you wouldn't believe the sort of thing they bring back."

For a moment Maigret wondered . . . Of course not! . . . For one thing, nothing had been stolen from the Colonel . . . and, besides, it didn't fit in with his character.

"Are you leaving?"

"I may be back soon. . . ."

He intended to wait until three A.M., and he had plenty of time ahead of him. Not knowing where to go, he prowled around again, sometimes in the guests' quarters and sometimes in the staff's; and as time went on, the comings and goings became more sporadic. He saw two or three couples returning from the theater, heard bells ring, met a waiter with a trayful of beer bottles, and another carrying up a complete meal.

Once, turning a corner, he ran into the chief reception clerk.

"You don't need me, Superintendent?"

"No, thanks."

The clerk was pretending to be there to help him, but Maigret was convinced he had come to keep an eye on him.

"Most of our guests don't come back much before three in the morning."

"I know. Thank you."

"If you need anything at all . . ."

"I'll let you know."

The man came back another time.

"I did give you the keys, didn't I?"

The superintendent's presence in the house was clearly making him nervous. Maigret nonetheless continued roaming around, found his way into a basement as large as a cathedral crypt, and glimpsed men in blue working in a boiler room that might have been a ship's stokehold.

Here, too, they turned around to stare at him. A clerk in a sort of glass cage was checking the bottles emerging from the wine cellar. In the kitchens, women were busy washing the tiled floor.

Another stairway, lighted by a ceiling lamp surrounded by wire netting, a swinging door, another glass cage in which there was nobody. The air felt cooler, and Maigret, pushing open a second door, was surprised to find himself in a street on the opposite sidewalk of which a man in shirt sleeves was lowering the blinds of the little bar he had noticed from the roof.

He was in Rue Magellan, and to the right, at the far end of Rue Bassano, lay the Champs-Élysées. In the next doorway, a couple were embracing; perhaps the man was the clerk who should have been in the glass cage?

Was this door watched day and night? Were the comings and goings of the staff monitored? Hadn't Maigret recently noticed a waiter in a white jacket cross the street and disappear into the *bistrot* over there?

Automatically he took mental note of all these details. When he returned to the bar, all the lights were out, the poker players had gone, and the waiters were busy clearing the tables.

There was no sign of the four Americans in the Empire-style lounge, which was deserted and looked like a silent chapel.

When he saw the bartender again, he hardly recognized him in his street clothes.

"Did the poker players leave?"

"I think they went up to Mark Jones's suite, where I guess they'll keep playing all night. . . . You're staying on? Good night . . ."

It was only a quarter past one, and Maigret went into the suite that had belonged to the late David Ward, where everything had been left as it was, including the scattered garments and the water in the bathtub.

He did not attempt to examine the place, but just sat down in an armchair, lighted a pipe, and stayed there drowsing.

Perhaps he had made a mistake in rushing off to Orly, Nice, Monte Carlo, and Lausanne. Incidentally, by this time the little Countess must be in bed in her sleeping car. Would she stay at the George V, as usual? Was she still hoping that Marco would take her back?

She was nothing, now, neither Ward's wife nor his widow, nor Marco's wife. She had admitted that she had no money. How long could she subsist on her furs and jewelry?

Had the Colonel foreseen that he might die before his divorce from Muriel Halligan had become final and he had been able to marry the Countess? That seemed unlikely.

The Countess didn't even have the consolation of joining the Lausanne club for unattached ladies, who in a restaurant would insist on dishes cooked without salt or butter, but who drank four or five cocktails before every meal.

Maigret did not attempt to reach any conclusion, to resolve any problem. He abandoned thought and let his mind wander.

Everything might depend on one little experiment. And even that would not necessarily be conclusive. It was just as well that the journalists who praised his methods didn't know how he sometimes went about things, for his prestige would undoubtedly have suffered.

Twice he almost fell asleep, waking with a start to look at his watch. The second time it was half past two, and to keep himself awake he changed his surroundings and went into number 332, where the only alteration made had been the prudent removal of the Countess's jewelry to the hotel safe.

No one, it seemed, had touched the bottle of whisky, and after about ten minutes Maigret rinsed out a glass in the bathroom and poured himself a drink.

Finally, at three o'clock, he made his way into the back regions again, just as a fairly tipsy couple were passing. The woman was singing and carrying in her arms, like a baby, an enormous white plush teddy bear that she must have bought in some nightclub.

He met a single gloomy-faced waiter who should have been retired, found his bearings, and went downstairs, too far at first, so that he landed in the basement, eventually returning to the still-vacant glass cage, and then breathing the cold night air of Rue Magellan.

The bar across the street had been closed for a long time. He had seen its blinds being lowered. The red neon light in the next street had gone out, and although the cars were still there, he saw no one on the sidewalk; only when he reached

151

Rue Bassano did he meet a passer-by, walking very fast, who seemed to be scared at the sight of him.

Fouquet's, at the corner of the Champs-Élysées, was closed too, and so was the brasserie opposite it. A hooker standing at the door of a travel agency muttered to him something he didn't understand.

On the other side of the avenue, where only a few cars were gliding by, two big shopwindows not far from the Lido were still lighted up.

Maigret must have looked like a somnambulist as he hesitated on the edge of the sidewalk trying to put himself into someone else's skin, someone who a few minutes earlier had killed a man by holding his head under the water in his bathtub and who had taken the same route as Maigret all the way from suite number 347.

An empty taxi coming along the avenue slowed down as it passed him. Would the murderer have signaled it to stop? Wouldn't he have reflected that this was too dangerous, since the police can almost always locate taxi drivers who have made a particular journey?

He let it pass, and considered walking down the same sidewalk toward Place de la Concorde.

Then he looked across the street again at the lighted café and the long, copper-edged bar. From a distance he could see the bartender serving beer, the woman at the cash register, and four or five customers sitting motionless, two of them women.

He crossed over, hesitated once again, and then went in.

The two women looked at him, preparing to smile; then they seemed to realize, without recognizing him, that there was nothing to be hoped for there.

Was this what had happened two nights ago? The man behind the bar looked at him, too, inquiringly, waiting for his order.

The hard liquor he had drunk had given Maigret a sour mouth, and he asked for a glass of beer.

Outside, two or three women emerged from the shadows to stare at him through the window.

One of them ventured briefly inside the café and then went back onto the sidewalk, presumably to tell the others there was nothing doing.

"Do you stay open all night?"

"All night."

"Are there any other bars open between here and the Madeleine?"

"Only striptease joints."

"Were you here the night before last at this time?"

"I'm here every night except Monday."

"And you, too?" he asked the cashier, who wore a blue woolen shawl over her shoulders.

"Wednesday's my night off."

The night in question had been a Tuesday. So they had both been there.

Maigret lowered his voice as he indicated the two young women: "Are they always here, too?"

"Except when they take a customer home to Rue Washington or Rue de Berry . . ."

The bartender was frowning, trying to place this strange customer whose face seemed somehow familiar. It was one of the two hookers who eventually recognized Maigret, and her lips moved in silent warning.

She was not aware that Maigret could see her in the

mirror, and kept repeating the same word, mouthing mutely like a fish; but the bartender, failing to understand her, stared first at her, then at the superintendent, and then questioningly back at her again.

Maigret ended up interpreting.

"Watch out!" he said.

And since the bartender seemed completely confused, he explained: "She's telling you I'm a cop."

"And is it true?"

"It's true."

Maigret must have looked funny as he said this, because the girl, after a second's embarrassment, could not help bursting into laughter.

*Those who
had seen something
and those
who had not,
or the art of mixing
one's witnesses*

"Why, no, Chief. I don't mind at all. I was expecting it, in fact I said as much to my wife when we went to bed."

Lucas had recovered his wits as soon as the telephone rang, but had probably not looked at the clock. He might not even have turned on the bedroom light.

"What time is it?"

"Half past three . . . Do you have a pencil and paper?"

"Just a minute . . ."

Through the window of the phone booth Maigret could see the washroom attendant asleep in her chair with her knitting on her lap, and he knew that upstairs in the bar they were talking about him.

"I'm listening."

"I don't have time to explain. Just follow my instructions exactly."

He gave them slowly, repeating every sentence to be sure there could be no mistake.

"See you soon."

"You're not too tired, Chief?"

"Not too bad."

157

He hung up, then called Lapointe, who took longer to wake up, possibly because he was younger.

"First go and have a drink of cold water. Then you can listen to me."

Lapointe, too, was given precise instructions. Maigret wondered whether to call Janvier, but the latter lived outside Paris and would probably take too much time finding a taxi.

He went upstairs again. The girl who had offered to wait for Olga outside her apartment on Rue Washington and bring her back had not yet returned, and Maigret had another glass of beer. The drink made him feel a little thickheaded, but that might be a help for what he had to do.

"Is it necessary for me to go, too?" pleaded the bartender across his bar. "Won't the two girls be enough? Even if he doesn't remember Malou, to whom he never spoke, he definitely won't have forgotten Olga, and she'll be here any minute. He not only bought her a drink and talked to her, but I thought he seemed ready to leave with her. Now, with that red hair and bust line of hers, you don't forget Olga in a hurry. . . ."

"I want you to be there."

"It's not for me that I'm asking, but for my partner, who'll have to be dragged out of bed. He'll really groan."

The girl who had gone to find Olga now returned with a flaming redhead proudly displaying a splendid bosom.

"That's him," her friend told her. "Superintendent Maigret. Don't be scared."

Olga still felt slightly mistrustful. Maigret bought her a drink and gave her and the other two instructions.

Finally he left the café alone and walked down the

Champs-Élysées in a leisurely way, his hands in his pockets, puffing gently on his pipe.

Passing the Claridge, he saw the doorman and nearly stopped to recruit him too. He didn't because he had noticed an old woman sitting on the ground a little farther on, leaning against the wall beside a basket of flowers.

"Were you here the night before last?"

She looked at him suspiciously, and he had to argue until he finally persuaded her after handing her over some money and repeating his instructions two or three times.

Now he could walk a little faster. He had assembled his cast. Lucas and Lapointe could arrange everything else. He almost took a taxi, but he would have got there too soon.

He reached Avenue Matignon, hesitated, then said to himself that the man had probably taken the route he was used to, a short cut through the Faubourg Saint-Honoré; he therefore passed in front of the British Embassy and the hotel where Philps was resting after the previous day's excursions.

The Madeleine, Boulevard des Capucines . . . Another uniformed attendant at the door of the Hotel Scribe, another revolving door, and a lobby less brightly lighted than that of the George V, and furnished in a more old-fashioned way.

He showed his card to the reception clerk.

"Is John Arnold in?"

A glance at the key rack, a nod.

"Has he been home a long time?"

"He came in about half past ten."

"Does that happen often."

"It's a little unusual for him, but with all this business he's had a pretty full day."

"What time did you see him come in last night?"

"Shortly after midnight."

"And the night before?"

"Much later."

"After three o'clock?"

"Possibly. You must know that we're not permitted to give out information about the comings and goings of our guests."

"Everyone is obliged to give evidence in a criminal case."

"Then you must speak to the manager."

"Was the manager here the night before last?"

"No. I won't speak without his permission."

The man was stubborn, stupid, and disagreeable.

"Put me through to the manager."

"I can't disturb him except for a really serious matter."

"This matter is so serious that if you don't call him immediately I'll run you in."

He must have realized that Maigret meant what he said.

"In that case I'll give you the information. It was after three o'clock, in fact after three-thirty, just before I had to send up to stop those Italians making such a noise."

He, too, got his instructions from Maigret, and the hotel manager had to be consulted after all.

"Now be kind enough to put me through to John Arnold. . . . Just ring his rooms. . . . I'll speak to him myself."

With the telephone in his hand, Maigret felt slightly nervous, because the game he was playing was a difficult and delicate one. He heard the ringing of the telephone in a room he did not know. Then the receiver was lifted. He asked, in a quiet voice: "Mr. John Arnold?"

And another voice replied: "Who is it?"

Still half asleep, Arnold had naturally answered in his native tongue. "I'm sorry to disturb you, Mr. Arnold. This is Superintendent Maigret. I'm at the point of arresting the murderer of your friend Ward and I need your help."

"Are you still in Lausanne?"

"No, in Paris."

"When do you want to see me?"

"Right away."

There was a pause, a second's hesitation.

"Where?"

"I'm downstairs in your hotel. I'd like to come up and talk to you for a minute."

A new silence. Did the Englishman have the right to refuse such an interview? Would he do so?

"Do you want to speak to me about the Countess?"

"About her, among other things . . ."

"Did she travel with you? Have you brought her along?"

"No . . . I'm alone."

"All right . . . Come up."

Maigret hung up, relieved.

"Which suite?" he asked the clerk.

"Five fifty-one. The bellhop will take you."

Passages, numbered doors. They met a single waiter, and he, too, knocked at the door of number 551.

Arnold, puffy-eyed, looked older than when the superintendent had met him at the George V. He was wearing a black dressing gown with a floral pattern over silk pajamas.

"Come in. Excuse the untidiness. What did the Countess tell you? She's a hysterical creature, you know. And when she's been drinking . . ."

"I know. . . . Thank you for letting me come to see you. It's

161

in everyone's interest, isn't it, except the murderer's, that this case be cleared up quickly. . . . I heard that you went to a lot of trouble yesterday with the English solicitor to get Ward's inheritance settled."

"It's very complicated," sighed the pink-cheeked little man.

He had ordered tea from the waiter.

"Will you have some, too?"

"No, thanks."

"Anything else?"

"No. To tell you the truth, Mr. Arnold, it's not here that I need to see you. . . ."

Although pretending not to look at him, Maigret was watching the other man's reactions as he spoke.

"My men at police headquarters have made certain discoveries that I would like to bring to your attention."

"What discoveries?"

Maigret gave no indication of having heard.

"I could, of course, have waited until tomorrow morning to send for you. Since you are the person who was closest to the Colonel and the most devoted to him, I thought you would forgive me for disturbing you in the middle of the night."

He was as bland as possible, speaking in the slightly embarrassed tone of an official faced with an unpleasant duty.

"In cases like this, time is of the essence. You yourself stressed the importance of Ward's affairs, the repercussions his death is sure to have in business circles. If you wouldn't mind getting dressed and coming along with me . . ."

"Where to?"

"To my office . . ."

162

"Can't we talk here?"

"That's the only place I can show you my evidence and consult you on certain problems."

This went on for a little longer, but eventually Arnold decided to get dressed, moving around between living room, bedroom, and bathroom.

Not once did Maigret utter the name Muriel Halligan, but he talked a lot about the Countess in a half-serious, half-joking tone. Arnold drank his scalding tea. Despite the time of night and the prospective destination, he dressed with his usual care.

"I suppose it won't take long? I went to bed early because tomorrow I've an even busier day than today. You know that Bobby, the Colonel's son, has come over with a friend from his college? They are staying here."

"Not at the George V?"

"I thought this was preferable, considering what happened there."

"You were absolutely right."

Maigret didn't rush him, quite the reverse. It was important to give Lucas and the others time to do all they had to do and get the stage set.

"Your life is really going to change, isn't it? How long had you actually been with your friend Ward?"

"Nearly thirty years . . ."

"Going around with him everywhere?"

"Everywhere . . ."

"And now, all of a sudden . . . I wonder if it was because of him that you never married. . . ."

"What do you mean?"

"If you'd been married you would have been less free to

accompany him. . . . In short, you sacrificed your personal life to him. . . ."

Maigret would have preferred to handle things differently, to stand face to face with the plump, neat little man and tell him frankly:

"Now let's have it out! . . . You killed Ward because . . ."

The unfortunate thing was that he did not know exactly why, and the Englishman would probably not have batted an eyelash.

"Countess Paverini is arriving at the Gare de Lyon at seven o'clock. . . . She's on the train right now. . . ."

"What has she told you?"

"That she went into the Colonel's rooms and found him dead."

"Have you summoned her to police headquarters?" He frowned. "You're not going to keep me waiting till she arrives?"

"I don't think so."

At last they walked together to the elevator, and Arnold automatically pressed the button.

"I've forgotten to take a coat."

"I don't have one, either. It's not cold, and we'll only have a few minutes' ride in a taxi."

Maigret didn't want to let him go back to his room. Soon, when they were in the cab, a detective would give it a thorough search.

They crossed the lobby too quickly for Arnold to notice that a different clerk was at the reception desk. A taxi was waiting.

"Quai des Orfèvres."

The boulevards were deserted. Just a couple here and

there, and a few taxis, most of them on their way to railroad stations. Maigret would not have to continue playing his unpleasant role and wondering if perhaps he was on the wrong track much longer.

The taxi did not drive into the courtyard, and the two men went on foot past the policeman on guard, and under the stone vault where the air was always colder than anywhere else.

"Do you mind if I lead the way?"

The superintendent walked ahead, up the massive ill-lighted staircase, pushed the frosted-glass door, and held it open for his companion. The huge corridor onto which the doors of various departments opened was empty, and only a few lights were on.

Just like hotels at night, Maigret thought, remembering all the corridors along which he had wandered that evening.

He said aloud, "This way . . . please go ahead."

He did not show Arnold straight into his own office, but into the inspectors' room. He himself stood back, because he knew what the Englishman was going to see when he went through that door.

One step . . . another step . . . a pause . . . He was aware of a shudder running down his companion's back, as though the man was repressing an impulse to turn around.

"Go ahead, please."

He closed the door and found the stage set just as he had imagined it. Lucas was seated at his desk, apparently very busy writing a report. At the opposite desk young Lapointe sat smoking a cigarette, and Maigret noticed that he was the palest of all. Had he understood that the superintendent was playing a difficult and possibly dangerous game?

Lined up against the walls, sitting on chairs, were figures and faces as motionless as waxworks.

These silent actors had not been placed at random, but in
a deliberate order. First came the night waiter on duty on
the third floor of the George V, his coat open over his black
trousers and white jacket. Then a uniformed bellboy. Next a
little old man with a peevish expression, the one who should
have been on duty in the glass cage beside the back door on
Rue Magellan.

These seemed the most uneasy, and they avoided looking
at Arnold, who could not have failed to recognize them, the
first, in any case, and the second because of his uniform.

The third of them could have been anybody; it didn't matter. Next came Olga, the redhead with the big bosom, who
was chewing gum to steady her nerves, and the girl friend
who had picked her up outside the apartment on Rue
Washington.

Finally the bartender, wearing an overcoat and carrying a
checked cap, the old flower vendor, and the reception clerk
from the Scribe.

"I suppose you know all these people?" Maigret said.
"We'll go and sit in my office and hear their evidence one at
a time. Have you the written statements, Lucas?"

"Yes, Chief . . ."

Maigret pushed open the communicating door.

"Please come in, Mr. Arnold."

The man stood unmoving for a moment as though rooted
to the floor, his eyes intently fixed on Maigret's.

Above all, Maigret must not avert his gaze, but maintain
his air of self-assurance.

He repeated, "Please come in."

He lighted the green-shaded lamp on his desk and pointed to an armchair opposite his own.

"You may smoke if you like."

When he looked at Arnold again, he realized that the latter had not stopped staring at him in unmistakable terror.

As naturally as possible, he filled his pipe and began:

"And now, if you don't mind, we will call in the witnesses one by one, to determine your movements from the moment when, in Colonel Ward's bathroom . . ."

And as he deliberately stretched out his hand toward the electric bell, he saw Arnold's prominent eyes grow moist, and his lower lip quiver as though with a sob. The man did not cry. Swallowing to ease the tension in his throat, he said in a voice that was painful to hear: "There's no need. . . ."

"You confess?"

A silence. Arnold's eyelids flickered.

And then something happened that was practically unprecedented in Maigret's career. He had been so tense, so acutely anxious, that his whole being suddenly relaxed in a manner that betrayed his relief. Arnold, who had never taken his eyes off Maigret, was stupefied at first, then he frowned and his face turned ashen.

"You . . ." He could hardly get the words out. "You didn't know, did you?" Finally, as he grasped the whole thing:

"They hadn't seen me?"

"Not all of them," Maigret admitted. "I'm sorry, Mr. Arnold, but it was better to get it over with, don't you think? It was the only way. . . ."

Hadn't he spared him hours, whole days, perhaps, of questioning?

"I assure you, it's better for you, too. . . ."

All the witnesses were still waiting next door, those who had really seen something and those who had seen nothing. By arranging them side by side in the order in which Arnold *might* have met them, the superintendent had given the impression of an unbreakable chain of evidence.

The weak links had, so to speak, passed muster under cover of the strong ones.

"I suppose I can let them go now?"

The Englishman made some effort to protest: "What's to prove, now, that . . ."

"Listen to me, Mr. Arnold. Now, as you have said, I know. You may retract your confession, and even pretend that it was extorted from you by brutal methods. . . ."

"I didn't say that. . . ."

"You see, it's too late to go back now. Up until now I didn't think it would be necessary to send for a certain lady who is staying at a hotel on Quai des Grands Augustins and with whom you had lunch yesterday. I can still do it. She'll take your place in front of me and I'll ask her enough questions to get an answer from her sooner or later."

There was an oppressive silence.

"Were you going to marry her?"

No answer.

"In how many days would the divorce have become final, thus obliging her to give up her claims to the inheritance?"

Maigret, without waiting, went to open the window. The sky was beginning to pale, and tugs could be heard hooting to their barges downstream from Ile Saint-Louis.

"Three days . . ."

Had Maigret heard? As though uninterested, he opened the communicating door.

"You can go home, all of you. I don't need you any more. You, Lucas . . ."

He had hesitated between Lucas and Lapointe. Seeing the latter's face fall he added: "And you, too . . . Come in, both of you, and take down his statement."

He went back into his office, chose a clean pipe, and filled it slowly, looking around for his hat.

"Now, if I may, I'll leave you, Mr. Arnold."

The Englishman sat huddled in his chair; he had suddenly aged, and every minute he seemed to be losing that sort of . . . that sort of what? . . . Maigret would have found it hard to express his thought. That indescribable quality of ease and self-assurance, that polish that distinguishes those who belong to a certain social class and who stay in grand hotels . . .

Now he was nothing but a mere man, a broken, wretched man who had lost the game.

"I'm going home to bed," Maigret told his colleagues. "If you need me . . ."

It was Lapointe who noticed that the superintendent, as he went by, laid his hand for an instant, as though absent-mindedly, on John Arnold's shoulder; and the young policeman's eyes took on a troubled look as they followed his chief to the door.

*Noland*
*August 17, 1957*